Praise

'Pip Adam is one of my favour
favourite book. Hurtling through
immediately gripped my heart is literature.
A powerful work of social commentary, a bodily exploration and a feat of imagination, all written with Adam's trademark poise: this is the genre-bending book of the year.'
—Laura Jean McKay

'Every now and then, you are lucky enough to come across a book so inventive, so thrillingly odd, that you struggle to stop thinking about it. *Audition* did that for me...A profoundly moving journey through ideas of incarceration and isolation. Adam trusts her reader to spot the trail of clues she drops before revealing all, and it makes for an exhilarating time.'
—Sian Cain, *The Guardian*

'Uncanny and astounding...in parts sci-fi, absurdist, fabulist, social realist...readers may find themselves equal parts unmoored and floored by this thrilling novel. I haven't stopped thinking about it.'
—Deborah Crabtree, *Books+Publishing*

'A blend of space opera and social realism, [*Audition*] is a fine example of Pip Adam's ingenuity and imagination.'
—Angelique Kasmara, *Aotearoa New Zealand Review of Books*

'Audacious, inventive and radical...A fearsome intellect underpins Pip's work, and *Audition* is threaded with astute psychological insights, but there is also absurdism and humour, erotica and brain candy, and pop culture references aplenty.'
—Sarah Laing, *Newsroom*

'*Audition* is in the great tradition of *Pedro Paramo* by Juan Rulfo or *The Invention of Morel* by Adolfo Bioy Casares – brief books that carry the weight of much longer volumes and are at once hallucinogenic, convincingly imagined and demanding your attention. It loses nothing by comparison with its antecedents.'
—Paul Little, *North and South*

A catalogue record for this book is available
from the British Library.

First published in New Zealand in 2023 by Te Herenga Waka University
Press, and in Australia by Giramondo Publishing.

First published in the United Kingdom in 2023 by Peninsula Press.

400 Kingsland Road
E8 4AA
London
peninsulapress.co.uk

Printed in Great Britain by CPI Group (UK) Ltd, Croydon

Cover design by Jo Walker

2 4 6 8 10 9 7 5 3 1
ISBN-13: 9781913512415

Audition

Pip Adam

PENINSULA PRESS, LONDON

For Brent, Bo and Coco

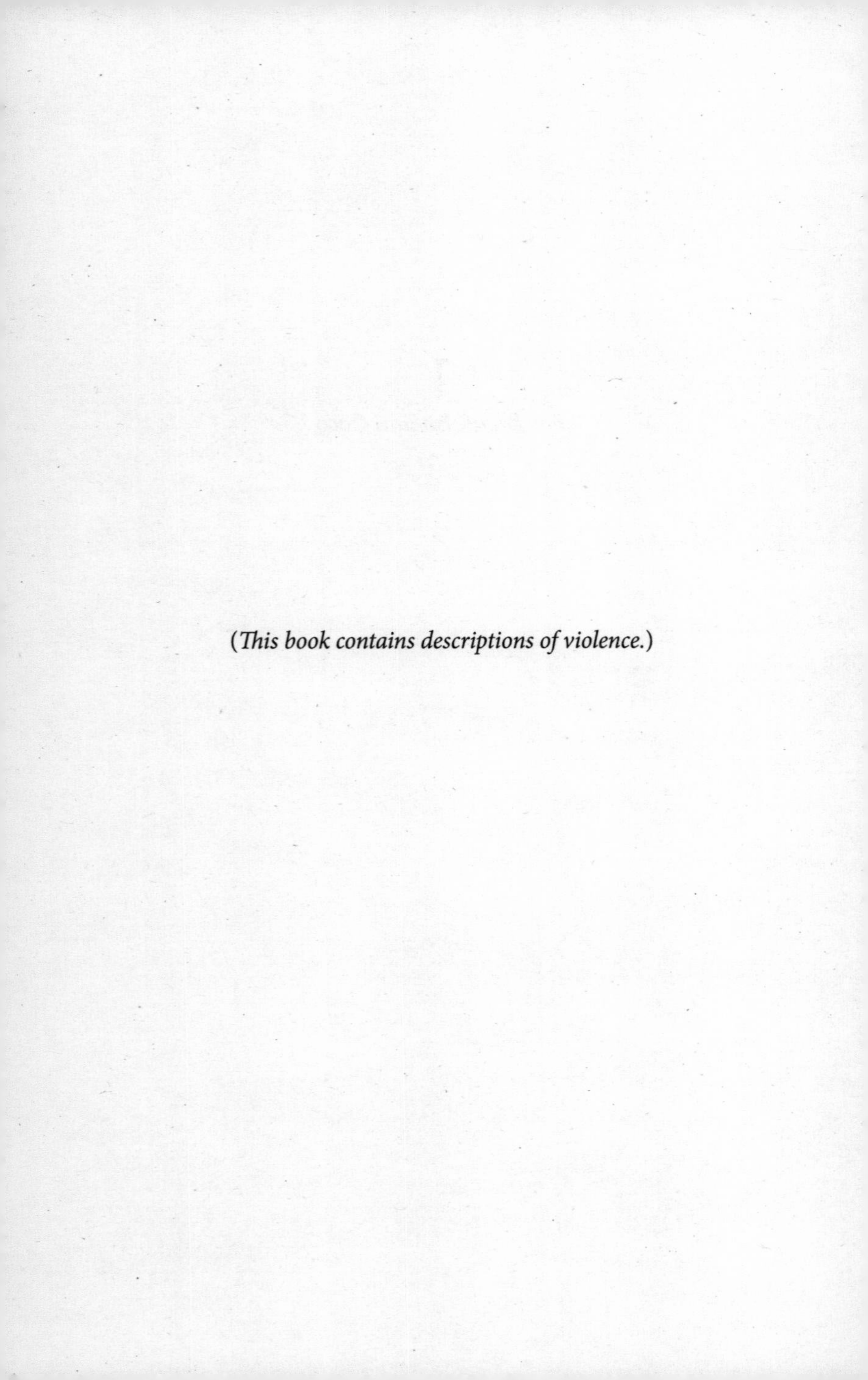

(This book contains descriptions of violence.)

1

Giant looks in the mirror and sees nothing.

Donda West

in the spacecraft
Audition

'I'm in the basketball court,' Alba says. 'Wedged between the floor and the ceiling.'

'I'm in a hallway,' Drew says. 'Unable to move. Pushed into a corner bent over and it's hard to breathe.'

'I'm stuck in the last room I could fit in,' Stanley says.

'We all are,' Alba and Drew say.

'We all are,' Stanley agrees.

'I feel like there used to be more room,' says Stanley. 'Like before this. I feel like I want to say, *This is a beautiful ship.*'

'I want to say,' Alba says. 'They have done a really nice job of building this . . . I want to say, spacecraft.'

'I want to say Audition,' Drew says. 'I feel like I want to say, They have done a good job of building this beautiful spacecraft called *Audition* and we are all lucky to be inside her.'

'And we only need to whisper to say it,' Alba whispers. 'Whisper it into the walls because *Audition* hears us and turns our noise into speed and steering . . .'

'. . . and air and gravity.'

'You can hear me and I'm only whispering,' Stanley whispers.

'We all are,' Drew whispers.

'We all are,' whispers Alba. 'And it is perfect. They did a good job of building the beautiful spacecraft *Audition*.'

'I think we all think we are going to die,' Stanley says.

'But really,' Alba says. 'What would we know?'

'It would be better if we took a moment to be really grateful for this beautiful spacecraft which used to be so perfect for us.

Which was built especially for us. When we got too big for Earth.'

'We were big on Earth,' Drew says.

'Too big,' Alba says.

'And now we're too big for the spacecraft *Audition*,' Stanley says.

'I think we're just not looking at it right,' Drew says. 'I think really, we're stupid and probably, there's nothing wrong with the ship and the circumstances we find ourselves in.'

'Bent over.'

'Painfully trapped.'

'A bird in an egg,' Stanley says.

'A foetus in a uterus,' Alba says.

'Waiting for something magnificent,' Stanley says.

'Also,' Alba says. 'We might still be growing.'

'Also,' Drew says. 'Gravity keeps humans small.'

'Not us. Not all of us in this ship. Earth's gravity did nothing for us.'

'We were inhumanly tall on Earth,' Stanley says. 'The classroom was outside – the roof was the sky. We towered over the teachers.'

'But,' Drew says, 'Earth's gravity, that seemed to have abandoned us so completely, cared infinitely more deeply than the spacecraft *Audition*'s fake gravity powered by the sounds of us living.'

'Why do we have a basketball court?' Stanley says.

'To play basketball?' Alba says.

'There are eighteen of us on the ship,' Stanley says. 'And five in a basketball team. Is the basketball court even for playing basketball?'

'Plus reserves,' Drew says.

'But still,' Stanley says. 'Even a child could see this would happen.'

'The growing again?' Alba says.

'The fast growing again,' Stanley says.

'You can feel the extent of the ship if you feel for it,' Drew says. 'There are eighteen of us on a ship the size of a small city. There's room for 10,000 normal-sized humans, 20,000 at a pinch. We were big. But not 1,000 times bigger than a normal-sized human.'

'Even a child could see it would happen if we stopped talking,' Stanley says. 'That if the gravity of a planet could only barely keep us at bay, in the engineered gravity of a spacecraft powered by sound if we stopped talking we would grow again – fast. But what would I know.'

'The people who built the ship did an amazing job.'

'Fuck.'

'Are you all right?' Stanley asks.

'I tried to sigh,' Alba says. 'But that banged my head into the roof.'

'We really do, now, have the strength to destroy the whole beautiful ship and now we have it we don't want it,' Stanley says. 'And then where would we be? If we put an end to the spacecraft *Audition*?'

'Maybe better,' Alba says. 'Maybe better to die in space than to grow and grow until your body explodes the ship anyway and you die in space anyway.'

'But maybe the ship will hold and our lungs will be crushed as our bodies run out of room finally. Us and the others.'

'Maybe, somewhere else in the ship, one of us is already out of control – having made a decision – on the verge of pushing the walls of the ship out into the darkness of space.'

'Shh,' Drew says. 'Listen.'

'Sound travels differently now we're all stilled and jammed up into corners and walls. It seems to be enough to keep the ship going but it's also muted.'

'Our bodies are so much bigger, they're dampening all the metallic that the ship used to make. All the high-pitch and ting of our huge boots when we walked down the corridors – the swish of the doors has stopped too.'

'How long has it been?'

'I'm not sure.'

'It started slowly,' Alba says. 'Like, these things always do – aided by a healthy hope that it isn't happening at all, a hope that kept everything at bay, made orderly decisions possible and then – it happened very quickly.

'All of us seeing all at once that all of us were growing again, very fast and before all of our eyes.'

'Like the steady roll of a train coming into a station getting clearer as it gets closer, as it gets bigger – so apparent in its inability to stop.'

'And we all dropped everything we were holding or doing or controlling and ran, in all directions towards wider, more open spaces. Some of us pushing others of us out of the way.'

'We were giant on Earth and it was terrifying – for everyone,' Alba says. 'But not like this.'

'We could see each other growing. In front of us,' Drew says. 'The beautiful ship *Audition* was built big to accommodate us but not now. Now we are twice as big as we were when we arrived.'

'Three times.'

'Six cubits and a span, on Earth,' Drew says. 'At least eighteen feet tall now.'

'I had room in the basketball court to start with,' Alba says. 'So much room I thought, maybe, we'd all overreacted. But now, I'm bent over from the part of my back that is just below my shoulders. My knees are sitting on either side of my head.

I'm pretty sure, maybe, that something inside me is broken, or disconnected, or at the very least cut off from circulation so it will need to be amputated, if I ever get medical help. But what would I know?'

'There's no help coming,' Stanley says. 'Because there's no help needed because everything is fine.'

'Someone knows how to fix this,' Drew says.

'Not anyone on this ship,' Alba says. 'We're all stupid. But someone in charge. They made a wonderful job of the ship.'

'If the people in charge had wanted us dead, they would have killed us on Earth,' Stanley says.

'There have been a hundred ships a day for nearly two years,' Drew says. 'The ships radiate out from all over the Earth's surface into endless space. A new astrology.'

'If they'd wanted us dead, they could have killed us on Earth and burned our bodies.'

'The fires would have raged all over the world. Lighting the night, melting the ice.'

'So,' Stanley says, 'probably they couldn't have burned our bodies.'

'But,' Alba says, 'this is also upsetting. Think of all the normal-sized people sad and powerless against the unforgiving nature of space.'

'They were good to us,' Drew says. 'Kind, when the growing on Earth started.'

'Sound travels differently now we're all stilled and jammed up into corners and walls. It seems to be enough to keep the ship going but it's also muted.'

'The ship is perfect.'

'My left eye,' says Alba, 'can just see out a skylight that was large when I first got on the spacecraft *Audition* but is small now. I can see the darkness and the stars, and they are beautiful, and I'm thinking again about breaking out but I can hear you talking through walls. The sound more like touch now we are all squashed so close to the walls, almost part of the walls.'

'I was saying, she came in the door and said, *Hello, Christina. It's a beautiful day. Isn't it the most beautiful day*?' says Stanley.

'I said, *I guess*, then, *Yeah*,' Drew replies. 'And she wanted to know if I loved New York in the fall.'

'I was puzzled,' Stanley says.

'And we all laugh our new laughs. The laughs a body makes when it is squashed up into the corners of a room as it gets too big. The laugh a body makes at an in-joke, at a secret.'

'It was a most beautiful day,' Alba says.

'No,' Drew says. 'The beautiful day is not the right story. Nothing of any worth happened before the classroom. We need to talk a lot now. We need more oxygen for our bigger lungs and there is not more oxygen available so we are tired and in pain but our lives depend on the noise and we can't make noise with our bodies moving. So, we need to talk a lot more now – stopping talking was a mistake. But we need to talk the correct things. It isn't as noisy and, even though we are all sure there is enough sound to keep the ship going because the ship is that good, any gap in the conversation is possibly playing havoc with everything.'

'Shall we have a conversation about before the classroom?'

'No,' Drew says. 'I think we should talk – through the vents, through the walls – the three of us who have ended up sectioned off in this . . . burrow – unsure if anyone else is alone, almost positive we're the only ones left.'

'But not about before the classroom?'

'No,' Alba says.

'We were stupid to be quiet,' Stanley says.

'Maybe someone told us this – maybe in the classroom or

maybe in passing – but the mechanics of the ship have been tuned to a fine point. To balance out the quieter times with the noisier ones – in the time between boarding the ship and the second growing – we slept, like, for at least eight hours every twenty-four, we slept. Sure, sometimes during this time, when we were too big for Earth but the right size for the ship *Audition,* we needed to shout – shout up into the roof, at the walls, make the microphones shake.'

'We would stomp our feet,' Stanley says. 'And bang things and the power would rise.'

'But normally,' Alba says, 'the ship just listened and was content with the eight hours of quietness that fell over us as we slept. At least some of us were awake, walking around, flushing toilets, snoring, farting. It stored the power from the noisy day deep inside it. Mainly, this was our job on the ship *Audition* – to make noise. Even though we might have a sense now that back on Earth, before the classroom of trying so hard to be quiet, that is not a story we need to tell and that is not a thought that needs thinking about because, really, there was nothing before the classroom. We need to talk about the things from the classroom and I don't think the beautiful day in New York and the bookshop come from the classroom.'

'The bookshop.'

'Nothing matters or has any worth before the classroom. Remember the sense of excitement in the classroom, that everything in the ship would rely on us walking with purpose, speaking clearly, sometimes shouting, sometimes singing and stomping our feet. Now though, there's no dancing and all we can do is talk. Whisper into the walls. Mouths pressed up against walls pushing vibrations through the walls, feeling the conversation through our cheeks and the other soft parts of us. And talking about before the classroom and New York in the fall and how we got to the classroom or where is the help is too negative and now is not the time and it is what it is, and we need to stop thinking so much. The ship *Audition* is a beautiful ship. They have made a good job of the spacecraft *Audition*. And really what would we know?'

'We're bigger now,' Drew says. 'The story is, we must be making more noise just from our bodies.'

'Certainly,' Stanley says.

'But we're not eating,' Alba says. 'There's nothing happening to make any noise – there's no machinery going to make any noise.'

'But our breathing,' Drew says. 'The story is – our breathing.'

'Yeah,' says Stanley. 'Our breathing is huge – powerful and loud.'

'Eventually though,' Alba says. 'The breathing won't be enough.'

'They made such a good job of the spacecraft *Audition*,' Stanley says.

'We are so lucky that they made such a good job,' Drew says. 'That our breathing is enough.'

'Eventually though,' Alba says. 'Nothing's going to be enough.'

'Except us,' Stanley says. 'We will be too much.'

'How many others are there?' Alba says.

'I haven't heard from anyone for ages,' Drew says.

'Maybe they're somewhere else,' Stanley says. 'The spacecraft *Audition* is built in three huge wings which are oblongs joined at one of their short ends. Spokes around an almost imperceptible bridge. Everything about the spacecraft *Audition* is designed to amplify any noise made in the spacecraft *Audition*.'

'Maybe,' they say together.

'It's totally possible they're out of earshot,' Drew says.

'It's a huge ship,' Alba says. 'A beautiful ship.'

'We have seen the ship once from the outside, as we walked toward it across the grassed plain, but none of us can fathom the entire extent of the ship now. It was lost to us the minute we came inside its huge rooms and its warren of hallways and its smaller rooms and the gardens and the primary colours on every wall – loud in design to remind us to be loud in voice.'

'And we disobeyed and stayed quiet.'

'We were stupid to stay quiet.'

'Are you still getting bigger?' Alba says.

'I can't tell,' says Stanley. 'It's days since I ran out of any room to grow into. Since I got stuck.'

'Stuck,' Alba says. 'But that can't be right. The story is we chose this space. This is the biggest room so there is no reason for me to go anywhere else. But really – and I'm trying now – I can't move. But that can't be right. I'm trying to move a finger and I can move that. I could move, probably any part of me but only a tiny way. At first, I got myself into all sorts of trouble repositioning to get comfortable and then finding, after a time – a few hours maybe – that there was no way out of the reposition.'

'We are stupid,' Drew says.

'Are you still getting bigger?' Alba says.

'I can't tell,' says Stanley.

'We're lucky we're safe,' Drew says.

'We are,' Alba and Stanley say.

'What would the physics be?' Alba says.

'I guess when we stopped talking, started creeping about there was less noise which meant maybe the gravity was less which was why we grew again – fast. But we're talking again now.'

'But sound travels differently now we're all stilled and

jammed up into corners and walls. It seems to be enough to keep the ship going but it's also muted.'

'It's enough to keep the ship going.'

'None of us really knew anything about physics though,' Alba says. 'I thought it in the classroom. I can see myself now, sitting in the classroom thinking, *No one here is an engineer.*'

'But what would we know?'

'Like really.'

'There's enough noise to keep the ship going,' Alba says.

'We should have smashed them.'

'What?' Alba says. 'Who said that?'

'We'll be fine,' Stanley says.

'Do we like fall in New York?' Alba says. 'Before the classroom we did think we could get the Christmas mailers out on Monday – we promised.'

'Nothing matters before the classroom. So, you do the maths.'

'Wasn't it the most beautiful day though?' says Alba. 'The day before we grew? Before the classroom?'

'Think about it and just forget about it.'

'We've been very lucky,' Alba says. 'The beautiful days were the days after we grew – our time in the classroom. Getting ready for the spacecraft *Audition*.'

'There is plenty of noise,' Drew says, 'The acoustics of the ship haven't changed. We only have to whisper and you can hear it for miles – throughout the whole wing. The ship is built like a huge amplifier. So, it can get as much energy as possible from the sound. Before all this it was always noisy. We made more noise than the normal-sized people because our bodies were bigger but we had big ears as well, so it was all scaled up. It had only been used for torture before but it worked for travel as well. The spacecraft *Audition* was designed completely to be the noisiest it could possibly be. There is no way the ship could be quieter and it is beautiful. We were never alone in a noisy place. We were stupid to be quiet in the face of the beauty of the spacecraft *Audition*. If we had kept talking, like they showed us in the classroom, we wouldn't have grown – the fast, second growing would not have happened. And now maybe we are the only ones left. Sometimes if we listen hard and the conditions are right we might think we can still hear others, in other wings, further apart. The ship really is huge.'

'They really have done a nice job of the ship.'

'The ship is beautiful.'

'At least it was before we started growing again and before we got stuck and the shit started piling up and the sweat started eating away at the wall finishes.'

'It was beautiful.'

'The people who made the ships were very, very smart.'

'They made a beautiful job of the ships.'

'It really is a lovely ship,' Stanley says. 'We all think it at the same time.'

'The acoustics of the ship haven't changed. So,' Drew says, 'when we say, *It really is a lovely ship*, everyone can hear it – possibly all over the ship – even though we can only whisper it now, into the walls. Alba can hear it and so can Stanley and me, I can hear myself saying it. Maybe it was something about our breath that makes us all think of the beautiful ship at once. Maybe we make some imperceptible noise when we think about the beauty of the ship which has become perceptible now we are so much bigger than we had been.'

'We haven't heard from anyone on Earth for a long time.'

'And this is why it feels like we all think of it at the same time. The imperceptible noise we make when we think it – made perceptible in our bigness and the quieter ship.'

'Huh?' says Alba.

'I like the way the walls shine,' says Drew.

'It must look beautiful from outside,' Alba says.

'I like the way the walls shine,' Stanley says.

'Yeah,' Alba says. 'The walls are pretty beautiful. They sure did make a good job of the ship.'

'When you think about it,' Drew says. 'We're kind of really lucky.'

'They could have killed us,' Stanley says. 'Set us alight.'

'So true,' Alba says. 'I was just thinking that before.'

'We all were,' says Stanley. 'I also like the way the doors work. Those are some good doors.'

'Such great doors,' Drew says.

'Maybe it's Friday,' Alba says.

'Greek roasted fish with vegetables salad day!' Drew and Stanley say.

'The story is: Monday is vegan superfood buddha bowl day,' Drew says. 'And I will list the story of the week's menu – as a gift, like a song, or entertainment. But really as fuel.'

'Monday is vegan superfood
buddha bowl day

Tuesday is Greek roasted fish
with vegetables,

Wednesday feels like it should
be buddha bowl again but
it's avocado, tenderloin,
boiled eggs and almonds in a
microwave bag.

'Talking is good,' Alba
says. 'That's what I think, but
probably we all think that.'

'We were stupid to stop
talking,' Stanley says. 'The
sneaking around, the being
quiet. We are stupid but that
was our dumbest idea. That
any act of protest would hurt
anyone but ourselves.

Thursday is a slice of cheddar cheese,

Friday is California roasted sweet potato kale salad,

Saturday is an eggplant or asparagus or one of the clean fifteen.

Talking is good. For the energy to keep us going, to keep the noise coming. Talking for talking's sake. The stories.'

'We left Earth's atmosphere on the third day. Earth wanted us close for a few days to make sure everything was working.'

Sunday's meat,' Drew says. 'Red meat chased and lightly broiled. It isn't often we are lost for words but if it feels like there isn't anything else, we can say things about food.'

'Because there's no weather,' Stanley says.

'I am looking out the skylight and there is no weather,' Alba says.

'I'm moving,' Stanley says.

'There was mostly porridge,' Drew says.

'But sometimes smoothies,' Stanley says. 'And all the milks.'

'All the milks,' Drew says. 'And millet and quinoa and elk flakes and something nutty, and small seedy things, and toast.'

'Sometimes Stanley,' Alba says, 'I will try this. Thinking, surely there is a way to be slightly more comfortable and, then, getting myself more and more committed to the new shape until, finally, with nowhere else to go without doing some kind of damage, I stop, and often I am less comfortable than I had been and I will have to go

'I'm sure there was toast,' Drew says. 'I mean lentils. There was always a hearty lentil soup.'

'Peanut butter, marmalade, other jams, cheese – cottage and cream.'

'Probably some eggs,' Drew says.

'Eggs done all ways . . .'

'Boiled.'

'Yes.'

without doing some kind of damage, I stop, and often I am less comfortable than I had been and I will have to wait for something to go numb. I'm sure soon bits of me will die from lack of circulation. Up until now I've kept everything except my tonsils. I have had every part of me that I came into the world with and part of me wanted to keep it that way but another part thinks how much more room I would have if an arm fell off or a leg but then, if I think for just a bit longer, I realise how stupid I am being because then I would have to lie with a rotting part of my body, stuck, as it stayed the same size and I kept growing. For the most part now we should stay in the same position. Talking is better than thinking.'

'Boiled and cold,' Alba says.
'Yes.'
'Warm and cold – probably even devilled with avocado.'
'Yeah.'

'I could do the alphabet,' Stanley says.

'0, 1, 1, 2, 3, 5, 8, 13, 21 . . .'

'Wait,' says Alba. 'That makes sense to me but I don't know where we know it from.'

'I don't know it,' says Drew.

'We won't get very far,' Stanley says.

'I think actually that's as far as I can get,' Alba says. 'In my head. Without a piece of paper.'

'Other people are smart and good at maths,' Stanley says.

'You do the maths.'

'We're stupid.'

'And boiled,' Alba says. 'Breakfast on the ship was always lovely. They really did do a nice job with the food.'

'And one morning,' Stanley says, 'while we were sitting around having a lovely breakfast on the spacecraft *Audition,* Drew noticed Shirley was pulling at her top. It kept separating from her trousers every time she moved, or laughed, or even just by itself.'

'Did she put that in the dryer?' Drew says.

'We were, stupidly, not talking so Shirley couldn't say.'

'Shirley was eating an egg and fruit and two cups of matcha. They go in the dryer though, don't they?'

'Yeah,' says Drew. 'But did she put it in the dryer for longer than you're supposed to?'

'Shirley pulled her top down and mouthed, *What are you looking at?*' says Alba, 'and you pointed at the gap where her skin was showing.'

'I pointed to the gap,' Drew says.

'Shirley shrugged.'

'But everyone in eyeshot, everyone who was privy to the silent conversation, felt themselves for a moment. Put their minds in their shoes.'

'Were our shoes tight?'

'And thought about where their legs came to on the chairs.'

'I thought, *Maybe it's just Shirley*,' says Drew.

'*Maybe it's just a little bit.* You were eating an avocado. You were trying to look casual.'

'Avocados were also for breakfast.'

'But really,' Alba says, 'it changed everything in that moment. Everyone walked differently that day as they went about their day and we had a silent meeting where everyone wrote down and pointed hard at what they had written. We needed to stay firm. And Monica wrote, *We have no power – but to stay silent. To break the spacecraft* Audition. We were ready to die – on our own terms but we didn't die, we grew – fast and in front of each other and then we ran.'

'We were so stupid to stop making noise.'

'You win some and you lose some.'

'It was our time.'

'They were so kind to us in the classroom.'

'In the classroom they told us it was like learning to drive a car. Once the thing is going, once we were out of earshot from the Earth. Once we were going, they said there was very little to do and, actually, probably it took less acumen and training than driving a car. *You can all drive cars, can't you?* It was rhetorical but I had no idea if I could drive a car, I still don't. Nothing that happened before the classroom matters. *The main job*, they said, *is the maintenance. The cleaning and the cooking and the cleaning*.'

'I said, *Like prison?*' Alba says. 'In the classroom. Back on Earth.'

'And a teacher said, *A bit*, and the next day the class began with a fifteen-minute explanation of how the ship was not like prison.'

'Torren?'

'Another teacher.'

'Hillary maybe.'

'If you'd asked nicely enough for it, I bet they would have made a smoothie,' Drew says.

'But really,' Alba says. 'I had no idea if I could drive until Torren told us. I didn't need to know anything about before we got to the classroom until Torren told us.'

'What story is that?'

'Us before the classroom.'

'No, what is that story you're telling about Torren telling us? I don't know that story.'

'What story about Torren?'

'The one you were just saying.'

'What would I know though?' Alba says.

'What indeed,' says Stanley. 'It would be best if we talked about breakfast. And not that breakfast with Shirley and the top. Monday is vegan superfood buddha bowl. Monday is vegan superfood buddha bowl and they've done a good job of the ship.'

'I'm sure there was bread,' Drew says.

'No bread.'

'Peanut butter, marmalade, other jams, cheese – cottage and cream?'

'No. Eggs,' Drew says.

'Eggs done all ways . . .'

'Boiled.'

'Yes.'

'It's about lunchtime,' Stanley says.

'What is?' asks Alba.

'Now,' says Stanley. 'It's about lunchtime now.'

'Time has changed,' says Drew. 'From the minute we left the Earth's atmosphere all bets were off. All bets. Who knows where we are or what time it is?'

'It's about lunchtime. Just because we aren't eating doesn't mean we don't want to be eating. Don't need food. There is so much more of us though – maybe there's enough fat stored to keep us from dying.'

'Unfortunately,' Drew says.

'It's a hibernation,' Alba says. 'I see bears. There are two wolves inside us – a black wolf and a white wolf. We are bears – I am a polar bear and Stanley is a grizzly bear. Drew is the wolf. We should never have met – but I was hunting and I stumbled on a wolf. I was so far from home in a zoo wandering back and forward. In a PowerPoint in the classroom – there are two wolves inside us, and it is like hibernation – it's that natural. Cruising through a forest that is green – spring-loaded. Bursting with potential and the potential for potential. The ground. We all think we can smell it but probably we can't. The forest that has grown in the ship *Audition*. Probably I am remembering it wrong but I can feel it, coming up through my feet, the dampness of the spring soil. I am hot and out of the zoo. Spring is windy. That's what I think next, spring is windy. Autumn is still. I look out the skylight again and for real now – I'm awake – for sure but maybe not. One of my eyes looking out the skylight like it is a keyhole. So, there is a strange doubling of the dark and the bright things in the dark. I try to shut my other eye but it doesn't work because as I go to shut it my eyelashes sweep across the roof and it feels bad so I keep both my eyes open. My tears could flood the place. I am thinking this and I am saying what I think. We all are. To keep the beautiful ship *Audition* going. If there was a mouse. Has a mouse come on board with us? Has a bear? Are the wolves out of us? Is there a bear? Listen? Stop your rocking and listen. But don't go silent – we were so stupid to go silent. Make noise and listen. A bear,' Alba says.

'A beer?' Stanley asks.

'b-e-A-r,' Alba says.

'Less likely,' Drew says.

'A forest,' Stanley says. 'The creak of the trunks and the sweep of branches high above. Pines. But transplanted to a non-native environment – the wrong ecology. Watered by downpours instead of sea mists. Growing, growing. Too tall. Like us.'

'Were we in the wrong ecology?' Drew asks.

'It doesn't seem like the worst hypothesis.'

'Like octopuses,' Drew says. 'Nothing on Earth has DNA like octopuses. We can learn a lot from an octopus – adaptability. No one told any of us about our DNA. No one told us anything. There were papers being written but no one told us about us. No one told us but they told us about octopuses – adaptable. Bears are powerful, direct, outgoing.'

'ENTJ.'

'In the classroom it was that natural. The spacecraft called *Audition*.'

'I tried to read one of the papers but I didn't have a university library card or a password for the aggregated databases that published the paper.'

'I tried to talk to a doctor at the classroom but he didn't know anything. Just what he'd read.'

'Had he read the papers?'

'No, he had just read a newsletter. There had been a webinar. He was told that really, he just needed to say it was natural – like a bear, like an octopus. An otter – ESFP. But, I wanted to talk to him. *Well*, and he looked at his watch, *There are lots of other people to see*. I had to hold onto my temper. I was so big. When I got angry it was frightening to anyone around me.

So, *Okay*, I said. *Okay*. Really it was all fine and what would I know? Really.'

'A beer?' Stanley says.

'b-e-A-r,' Alba says.

'Less likely,' Drew says.

'The softest of pads on the spring-heavy ground that smells of damp and soil if you walk over it and sounds of the deepest throb of the planet if you are face down on it. Lying, feeling the damp soak through whatever you're wearing. A large bear, pigeon-toed lifting a foot claws-last slowly taking in this new world. Asking, *Am I still asleep? Is this a dream?*'

'We have measured our days by the sun and now there is no sun.'

'There is sun but it stays put and we are moving in a straight line away from it. It is always at our backs. Causing strange shadows like the lowest winter's morning or afternoon.'

'So, without being able to check a screen or a watch we have no idea how much time has passed. Maybe it has ceased passing. Since we stopped eating it is harder to tell. Our bodies were relatively reliable time mechanisms – hungry at certain times each day or at least hungry at certain distances from their last meals. But now we are hungry all the time. We slip sometimes in and out of dizzy sleep, but the sleep holds no order to it. It may have only been a day. This is a terrifying thought.'

'And sometimes we are wide awake.'

'We left the Earth's atmosphere on the third day,' Stanley says. 'Earth wanted us close for a few days to make sure everything was working.'

'That was a big risk,' Alba says, 'I overheard someone saying that – early on, when things were a bit loose, before the accidents. We were so big. We took up so much room, the idea of all that weight and height and human coming crashing to

Earth must have been scary for them. But what would we know?'

'And we laugh,' Stanley says.

'It's all pretty ridiculous,' says Drew.

'That's one of the hardest things about it. How stupid we looked and how stupid the whole thing was.'

'The size of us is stupid,' Alba says. 'People made big things for us. A big comb, a big shower.'

'People still make big things for us,' Stanley says. 'I don't think anything changed from the very start to the very end of us on Earth.'

'I think that was me that told you that,' Drew says.

'And me,' says Stanley.

'And me,' Alba says. 'We could ask for a comb but probably asking for, say, a vibrator was not okay. Anything private we needed, we had to improvise.'

'Anything,' Stanley said.

'I became intimate with myself in a way I never had been when I was my old size. I knew how much blood things held. How much earwax my ears made. How much hair fell out when I brushed it. All the things that came off me needed to be contained and disposed of. There was a lot of it.'

'More and more as I got bigger and bigger,' Alba says.

'Tablespoons turned into cups. Little wonder they wanted shot of us. People could drown in the amount of fluid that came off me over a month.'

'Normal-sized people could have drowned,' Stanley says.

'But people nonetheless.'

'I had to walk so far to get any benefit. I was probably physically fit – from carrying so much more of me around – but I stayed proportionally fat.'

'My legs needed to be big to hold the weight of me,' Stanley says.

'Elephants,' Drew says. 'Reliable, loyal, principled.'

'I didn't realise elephants were mammals,' Alba says. 'Now I say it out loud I'm not sure what I thought elephants were but I realise now that I never thought they were mammals. Maybe it's their skin. Is an alligator a mammal?'

'Alligator is not on the list.'

'Why are we talking about mammals?' Drew says.

'I'm not sure,' Alba says. 'But the story of how big things can get has quickly become limited to mammals.'

'Because you're one,' Stanley says.

'Have we had this conversation before?' Alba says.

'You had it with a normal-sized person,' Drew says. 'Torren maybe. I overheard it – at the classroom.'

'Me too,' says Stanley. 'You were sitting outside with our family.'

'Is Torren my family? Wait. Where is my family?'

'You towered over them, trying to stay low to the ground so you looked low. Our family was picking at the grass. You couldn't do that anymore. You were that strong. You could pull piles of soil out at a time. Then your family said, *Elephants have big legs. They have four big legs, because they are big.* You asked, *What about giraffes?*'

'A good point,' Drew says.

'*They're more like a horse*, your family said nodding, happy with themselves.'

'But they're mammals though,' Alba says. 'And I don't think Torren is our family. Once we got to the classroom, I don't think I knew any normal-sized people who weren't teachers.'

'Well,' Drew says. 'This family, which I think was probably not family but a teacher at the classroom, nodded and looked out over the space you and they were sitting near – the pitch that the classroom was in, the playing field. You were under a tree or at least you were in a place where a tree could have been and there were people everywhere walking in the park or there were no people there at all only us, only the giants in the classroom and the teachers and maybe it was a time between classes and you said, *But giraffes don't have big legs.* There was a small child looking at you so you lay down lower. And they said, *But they don't count, stupid.*'

'Why don't giraffes count?' Alba says.

'That's what you said,' says Stanley. 'And they said, *Because they're not as heavy as an elephant.*'

'But they're big,' Alba says.

'Tall,' Stanley says.

'What?' Alba says.

'They said giraffes were tall, not big.'

'Am I a giraffe or an elephant?' Alba asks. 'It's hard to tell and my back hurts. Are there any two-legged ones that are big?'

'To begin with, your family who was a teacher, maybe Torren, didn't know. They thought for a minute, pulled some more of the grass up, looked out on the park or the barren place that could have been a park where we lay in the elements at night and slept and thought about it and then they said, *Gorillas?* but it wasn't really a question because they knew we were stupid and you had no answers.'

'But gorillas get around on four really,' Alba says. 'Just cause they used the front ones like hands doesn't mean they don't also use them like legs.'

'And the teacher said we were so lucky – all of us – that we had come to the classroom when we did. That if we hadn't come to the classroom we wouldn't have stopped growing and who knew how much longer we would have been able to hold ourselves up if we'd kept growing,' says Drew.

'But had we stopped?' Alba says. 'At the classroom had we stopped?'

'You looked at your legs,' Stanley says, 'and I also looked at my legs. Our legs were lying out beside us. We were reclining, Roman-like, on our sides under the tree we wished was there. We're larger now than we had been on that day but that day we were larger than we had ever been. It took a bit of conceptualising to feel it. We felt the same in ourselves. But the world told us we were getting taller. Doorways, cars, shoes, a jacket that pulled our arm back as we walked down the New York street in fall. It was slow but steady. So slow. Almost imperceptible but some days we would go to put on our jacket and it wouldn't fit any more.'

'Did we have jackets?' Alba says. 'I think maybe Drew had jackets but you and me, Stanley, we only had grey, soft – but they got too small too.'

'There was pain with it but there was always pain,' Stanley says. 'Always new pain, some new way that life was uncomfortable. If we've learnt anything – it's that. Life is pain. So, the pain gave little sense of the growing. Unless it was directly related to the growing. When we first got to the classroom sometimes, we'd walk around barefoot because our shoes got tight. But the other pain, the one that came from inside us, was like a noise. That pain was not a good indicator of our size or of how far we'd grown. My feet were further away. That was an empirical truth. It only took a measuring tape or, in the absence of a measuring tape, anything of a constant length, to tell how much taller I was from the morning. In essence that was the problem I was facing. The world was of a constant size and we were not. Our whole life, since it began, had been our changing bodies coming into contact with the constant and unchanging.'

'What about dinosaurs?' Drew says.

'What about them?' Alba says.

'They walk on two legs.'

'Not very well.'

'Fine though,' Stanley says. 'Like they were quite alright at walking. Like some of the best alpha predators ever to walk the Earth were huge and on two legs.'

'You looked at the tree for scale – or where the tree could have been,' Drew says. 'And you thought, *Thank God I came to the classroom before I grew any bigger.* But our family-teacher had a point. Giraffes don't count and you were stupid to bring them up.'

'Aren't they more like birds?' Alba says.

'Huh?'

'The dinosaurs. Didn't they have feathers? Maybe they had bird bones.'

'The trainer started eating then. They had sandwiches from somewhere – maybe they had a bag. They were eating sandwiches in large mouthfuls and saying, *No. Dinosaurs have big bones. Realistically, their bones are the main thing we have, stupid. So, there's no question about it.* Our family was right, they were just trying to explain where we came from.'

'But,' Drew said. 'But, there are stones that show the feathers too. I saw them.'

'We'll all close our eyes and imagine ourselves in the classroom and look out over the park and watch the dinosaurs to see. Like there's a wrinkle in time somehow. Like the dinosaurs have just walked through and we aren't the largest thing on two legs anymore. We could kill the dinosaurs or tame them or enter into a friendly compromise. We don't know which and maybe there is some other way of being with the dinosaurs but we are stupid. We watch them now. In our mind's eye. Walk over the park, carefully picking their way through the people who don't even scream because not all big things are scary.'

'So, the sandwiches?' Stanley says. 'The story of the dinosaurs is making us too quiet. The story of the dinosaurs makes us too much in our minds, in our individual minds. It is selfish to tell the story of the dinosaurs in the park. Especially in the spacecraft *Audition* with the conversation running so low. The real is better than the make-believe. So, the sandwiches?'

'The family which was mine and yours and teachers and maybe Torren and not family said, *Do you want a sandwich?*' Alba says.

'What sort of sandwich?' Drew asks.

'A boiled egg,' Alba says.

'Like one slice of bread then butter, then some sort of meat substitute and some lettuce and a boiled egg and then more butter on another slice of bread?'

'No,' Alba says. 'A boiled egg. The eggs were in a small plastic container the type takeaways come in if you are working late at the independent bookstore called The Shop Around the Corner. I was hungry, so I said, *Yes please*, and they handed me the container. Our hands were big and the seal on the container was tight and the place where you get purchase on the lid to open it was normal-hand sized. Our not-family watched us. Then it got too hard to watch, too ugly, too frightening so they looked out on the park. I broke the lid.'

'We broke the lid.'

'I made it snap in two pieces. It made a loud crack and my family-teacher looked over in surprise then disappointment then snapped back to looking at the field.'

'We can't have nice things,' Stanley says.

'They are so kind to us,' Alba says. 'So very, very kind and we ruin everything.'

'Did you say sorry?' Drew says.

'I said sorry,' Alba says. '*All good*, our teachers said, but slightly too fast, because they are kind and we are not. *It's just an old container*, they said. *We can probably get another lid.* I lifted up the container, to show them that it, also, was broken. *Oh*, they said. *All good.* The egg sat in my hand. My hand wasn't that much bigger than theirs I had started with quite small hands. But the egg sat on my palm and there was still room on my palm. The teachers weren't looking. They would be happy once the egg was gone. But really, they were just happy it wasn't them. In the classroom, being around so many of us, it made them hyper-vigilant. No one wanted to be giant. Checking their height each morning.'

'One morning,' Stanley says, 'our teacher put on a pair of shoes and I could tell they felt quite tight, and that they were thinking, *Do these feel quite tight?* I was pretending to put on my own shoes but I was watching them, out of the corner of my eyes. They lifted them up and rolled the sole of them over the sole of their foot. I was supposed to see none of this. The shoe seemed like it should fit but maybe their foot was slightly bigger. They'd probably never rolled the shoe over their foot like that before. Then they put their hand in the shoe and pulled out a small nude sock – only half a sock really, probably less than that, just for your foot, so you can look like you're wearing bare feet under your shoe. It was the tiny sock that had made the shoe tighter. There was less room in the shoe for their foot when there was already a baby sock in it. There were several false alarms like this. So, it must have been slow. Subtle, and so slow. When it started before the classroom.'

'Nothing matters before the classroom it was our time.'

'It wasn't like a werewolf,' Drew says. 'I heard someone say that once.'

'It must have been creeping,' Alba says. 'Who told us that? About the creeping?'

'Not at all,' says Drew. 'And it wasn't steady. Some days were much worse than others. Sometimes I would sit down and then when I got up I'd bump something because it had happened in the meantime. Maybe I was a centimetre taller, maybe I was fifteen centimetres taller.'

'Before we came to the classroom, we were ringing up a sale and getting the Christmas fliers out on Monday because we had a paper due Friday.'

'It wasn't fast,' Alba says. 'I'm saying that as more of a question than a statement. This conversation about the growing and the creeping and the Christmas fliers and the paper is not a story from the classroom. No one talks about before the classroom in the classroom and we don't need to talk about it here. We were lucky to be brought to the classroom, we were lucky to be there.'

'Maybe that's why no one could be totally sure that it had completely stopped,' Stanley says. 'Because there was no story.'

'And we remember it again, it is bright in our minds now. The screaming. The running. The panic of that day in the spacecraft *Audition* when we realised what we'd done by being resistant. That we were growing again, faster than ever and in front of the eyes of everyone.'

'We were stupid to be quiet.'

'We are stupid.'

'What would we know?'

'It would be better if we finished the story – the classroom, the tree or the no tree, the sandwiches that were boiled eggs. Although it isn't a proper story. It's not a story from the classroom. It's a story about a lunch break and a lunch break is not a class.'

'It might be we have run out of the proper stories – that we lost them in the not-talking but this story – the tree, the eggs – has the shape of the stories we were taught by the teachers at the classroom. That other story – the 'before the classroom and the bookshop' is not the right shape of a story. So tell the container story.'

'We broke the lid and the container,' Alba said. 'They are so kind and we ruin everything and then a kid walked in, with a Walkman on. Maybe they were ten.'

'Were there children?' Stanley says. 'At the classroom?'

'On visiting day,' Drew says. 'Surely.'

'Visiting day?' Stanley says.

'We really do ruin everything,' Alba says. 'We've ruined this story. This is not a story. The story is, the spacecraft *Audition* is a beautiful ship and we are lucky to be here. What is the rest?'

'I am restless,' Drew says.

'We can feel it,' Alba says. 'Anyone, anywhere in the ship *Audition* can feel it. It happens, I will tell the story of it – so we aren't silent. Our bodies get restless – like there is a buzzing inside all our muscles – or maybe just our legs, or an arm – and we will try and move. Just a little bit at first. Then sometimes roughly, then sometimes we will rock back and forward and the ship will shift slightly in the air.'

'We were taught to go a long way away,' Stanley says. 'But there is no advised destination. We were adventurers. Setting out.'

'*Like Cook*,' Drew says. 'A teacher said it in the classroom. It didn't go down well.'

'Cook's a cunt,' says Stanley.

'Nobody wants to be compared to Cook. One of us, right at the back of the room where the *Like Cook* comment was made, let out an audible, *Ew!* and a few of us giggled. We were big.

Nothing we said was quiet. Even when we spoke under our breath to ourselves, it came out audible. Nothing we did was private. We were big and strong.'

'We weren't as strong as we thought we were,' Alba says. 'The story is, we are not as strong as we think we are.'

'And we are stupid so any strength is of no use at all.'

'Like Cook,' Drew says.

'Don't bother,' Alba says. 'We're all tired.'

'Hang on,' says Alba. 'This is one from before the classroom but it is the right shape, I am sure of it. Remember when he left us with the dog? He wanted to take her for a walk – she was wearing the white jumpsuit, they were about to meet. It was so hot.'

'It was winter,' Stanley says.

'No,' says Alba. 'No. It was a sunny day because love was in the air.'

'It was cold,' Stanley says. 'New York in the fall.'

'No,' Alba says.

'Yes,' says Stanley.

'This is painful,' Alba says. 'Not because I need to be told. Because I do need to be told, I am stupid but as soon as you said it, the first time – that it was cold – I knew I was wrong. Or that I remembered it wrong and a fear came over me, like from deep inside and I thought, *What else have we forgotten?* What else do we have wrong? Did maybe the dinosaurs never exist? Or the giraffes? Were there no children on visiting day? Were there no visiting days? Was maybe there never a happy moment. Have we always been this way?'

'It was winter,' says Stanley.

'It was winter, and the dog was named Rufus and I'm not even sure he wanted to be a senator.'

'Rufus.'

'Not Rufus,' says Alba. 'Christopher "Chris" Marshall. We worked so hard to get the meeting for him at the lady's lunch and he just handed us Rufus, *He's in a hurry I'm fine*, and left to meet her, for the first time in a white pantsuit which wasn't hers – in the end.'

'But it's not the end yet,' Drew says. 'Rufus and the white pantsuit is just the beginning and he promises he will make it to the next meeting.'

'There was a child there,' Alba says. 'That's where the kid was. We met the kid in the elevator and then he was her son and then they went for a walk. It wasn't us at all in the park. He must have told us when he got back, after the walk with the woman. What did we do? While they meet and are cute?'

'We walked Rufus.'

'We walked Rufus.'

'Were we quiet and has time passed?' says Drew.

'There is a noise,' Alba says. 'It isn't any of us. And all of us opened our eyes with a start. I wasn't asleep. I was staring at the floor but it felt like I was sleeping but I was not asleep. Our start made noise so we tried quickly to settle again so we could listen out for the next noise. Is the noise new?'

'We will have to listen to it while we make noise because we were stupid to be quiet.'

'It sounds like a door opening,' says Stanley. 'At least to me. To me it sounds like a door opening. But there is none of the attendant suck of a door opening or closing. Is it coming from outside?'

'I have twisted, slowly, slowly as carefully as I can but still trying to make noise with it so I can look out the skylight that used to be huge above me but is now small.'

'Are you squinting?'

'It is a light,' Alba says. 'But there is always a light of one sort or another. Space is meant to be dark but it is busy. When all you have to look at is space it starts to take on a shape, a rhythm. We have learnt to notice the shift in it. The way there is more than one shade of black. The way the stars move slightly as we move toward them. The way the ship moves to stay on course. I can always see when the ship has made a correction. None of us know where we are going. The spacecraft *Audition* knows. They have made a beautiful job of the spacecraft *Audition*. Something, though, has changed in the journey of the ship. I am sure of it. It is like a temperature rise or a small pain in a small part of my body. Something is different.'

'Can you see anything?' Stanley whispers.

'Shh,' Drew says. 'Well? Alba? Can you see anything?'

'Nothing,' Alba says.

'Feels different though?' Stanley asks.

'Feels different,' Alba says. 'The ship is large – huge.'

'Maybe it's just one of the others?' Stanley says. 'Making the noise. Maybe we are wrong that nothing's changed. What would we know? We're stupid.'

'Yeah,' Alba and Drew say.

'But we're not wrong. Something has changed. All of us are hoping it is someone from outside. Someone come to rescue us. *Surely, we have passed space stations?* We all think to ourselves. Surely, we can be followed. But we are alone in space. This is the truth of it. Alone and alone. No one is there and no one can get to us. But maybe. Maybe this is just a story they told us – so we committed, so we learnt everything we could. So, we worked hard and really, they were right beside us the whole way. But why would they lie? It is true – alone and alone. I am sure of it. It is all true. All of it. They were very kind to us and told us all the truth there was to tell and we were stupid to stop making noise because it broke the spacecraft *Audition* but not in the way we wanted – we grew fast and in front of each other. We were stupid and we are stupid. We are stuck and alone and now there is a noise and it is probably something breaking under the weight of us. Or something being forced open by the size of us. A panel somewhere swinging open. The final paper-thin barrier between us and the outside – and death. But what would we know?'

'Remember that day we met?' Drew says.

'Huh?' Alba says.

'All of us different sizes but all of us big. Some of us would have just got through a normal-sized door, some of us wouldn't have fitted under a normal-sized roof. The classroom was outside for us. It was summer – we would be gone by autumn. And beside the classroom were the tents where the teachers would meet and the storerooms with the food we would eat and the simulators of the spacecraft *Audition* and *Frequency* and *Echo* and all the other spacecraft.'

'Yeah,' Alba says. 'Yeah. It was a cold grey day.'

'It was summer,' Drew says. 'Bright.'

'The classroom was outside but maybe it felt like inside on a winter day,' Stanley says. 'The stadium that the classroom was in was big and the stands with the seats went high. High like a building in a busy city.'

'Like New York.'

'Like Chicago.'

'It was a beautiful stadium,' Drew says. 'They really made a nice job of that place. It was for sport and conventions and us.'

'The whole place was nice.'

'We're all supposed to keep our hair short. There is so much hair on us. But it's growing back now. We nod or make the intention to nod, a slight brush against the walls.'

'It is growing back now. Not fast like the rest of us.'

'We're not werewolves. But we have been stuck for a long time now – maybe weeks – so there was no chance to cut our hair, so our hair adds an extra rustle to the sound of us barely nodding our heads in agreement. Agreeing with Drew, playing at peacekeeper. Agreeing, yes, it was a beautiful place, so we don't need to litigate whether it was a sunny or overcast day.'

'Over cats,' Drew says. 'I always used to mistype it. So stupid.'

'Are you?' Stanley asks.

'No,' Drew says. 'I quite like cats. I don't feel like I've had too much of them by any stretch of the imagination.'

'Meerkats – ESTJ.'

'The sun's up,' says Alba. 'Or maybe it isn't. It is early in the year or maybe it is almost the end. There are three of us. I am sure. But maybe we are a city full of people going about our day but making it difficult for the lovers to meet. Or maybe I am by myself – under a tree, dressed as a girl waiting for a guy, for a prom where the theme is "Made for each other" or maybe I am really a girl waiting for a guy. But even when I try it out like this, I am certain there are three of us: Drew, Stanley and me. At the classroom we had to be told. The work we did there made us resonate at the perfect amplification. So, we were loud enough, at the right pitch to run the ship.'

'I was expecting a boot camp,' Drew says.

'One,' Alba says.

'But it was more like a talk.'

'Even though we were outside it smelt like a hotel,' Stanley says.

'Two,' Alba says. 'It was like self-help,' Alba says. Then, 'Three. And we all agree – one, two, three – there are three of us. The rest are gone. I am sure of it now and I know you are too.'

'I've never been to a life-coaching course,' Drew says. 'But it was like that. The chairs were set equidistant from each other – if there had been chairs. The toilet breaks – mandated and the food at set times.'

'The food was so good,' Stanley says. 'I'd love some of that food now.'

'Monday,' Alba says. 'Vegan superfood buddha bowl day. The teachers were all normal sized. And the special speakers. Remember how the stage swamped them? What did they eat? There must have been special plates of food where they ate. Like normal-sized plates.'

'You shouldn't call them that,' Drew says. 'They don't like "normal-sized".'

'There were uniforms,' Stanley says. 'I'm using my voice – as I whisper – trying to make it sound like we are all trying to remember – for suspense. But it is all as clear as day. Every day the special speakers told us the story of the classroom. Sometimes in the classroom we three sat together and recited the order of things. Like math. The truth of things. That was the story we were told. The story of the truth of things is: We are stupid. What would we know? Stupid is as stupid does. But, maybe. We were all thinking, maybe. Maybe if we came at it one more time something would break, like a wall under a battering ram. Wouldn't something give if we came again at the *this is the truth of things*?'

'It is what it is,' Stanley whispers. 'Now is not the time.'

'Monday is vegan superfood buddha bowl day etcetera.'

'Tuesday comes after Monday.'

'Nothing before the classroom matters so it's all good.'

'The spacecraft *Audition* is a beautiful ship. The spacecraft

Audition will protect us. They really have done a wonderful job of the spacecraft *Audition*.'

'What would we know?'

'We are stupid.'

'It would be better if we realised nothing before the classroom matters.'

'It would be better if we put down that pipe.'

'It would be better if we just agreed.'

'It would be better if we didn't make a fuss.'

'It would be better if we made noise.'

'They weren't called uniforms,' Drew says. 'They called them clothes. *These are your clothes*.'

'Please make sure these are the clothes you are wearing at all times.'

'Please don't wear any other clothes with these clothes.'

'Actually, give us your clothes from before and we'll look after them.'

'I am looking out the skylight and taking as deep a breath as I can,' Alba says. 'Am I getting bigger?'

'Where are the clothes we brought with us to the classroom now?' Drew says.

'Nothing before the classroom matters so now is not the time.'

'Remember The Shop Around the Corner though?'

'Fox Books was bigger.'

'Was there online shopping?' Alba asks.

'Not from The Shop Around the Corner.'

'Not even from Fox Books. Not yet.'

'Obviously, eventually, there was online shopping.'

'There was AOL,' Stanley says. 'Shopgirl. NY152.'

'Kathleen, George, Aunt Birdie, Christina – the Christmas mailers, the paper.'

'Someone invented a way to capture radio waves – to make them vibrate through wires and then someone found a way to make the wires carry all sorts of information and then there was the internet. . . '

'AOL.'

'AOL, and then there was http and then there was online shopping. But was there online shopping? If there was online shopping we could have brought our own new clothes when we got to the classroom. But surely there are more reasons to not buy our own new clothes.'

'The world is ending,' Stanley says.

'Not yet maybe,' Drew says.

'There was so much waste,' Alba says. 'But I am trying to outrun something. Also, did we have a credit card? Did we have credit on our credit card? Was it some kind of terrible mismatch where there was online shopping but no one had invented credit cards? Was I on an Atlantic crossing with Olympic athletes spying on my boss's son's fiancée, recording them with film and tape and at the same time surfing the net for material to make a T-shirt that would fit me.'

'But what would we know?' Drew says. 'We're so stupid.'

'We boarded the ship willingly,' Stanley says. 'It was Lorelei's idea maybe even. The ship to France, to the classroom. Before we left, Gus gave us a letter of credit to cover expenses upon our arrival. He was going to meet us there but then the credit was cancelled and we worked as a show girl and it's complicated.'

'More complicated than saying we are the fiancée of the man in a coma?'

'Much more complicated.'

'But we got on the ship to France willingly. And we got on the ship to the classroom willingly. And that ship was a truck.'

'The noise hasn't stopped,' says Alba. 'We are talking but

we can still hear it because maybe it is getting louder. The ship is still going in the new direction. But we aren't talking about that. We should stick with the truth of things. Forget about the ship to France and the truck and before the classroom and how we got to the classroom. It would be better if we remembered that before the classroom doesn't matter. Although, we also all know there is a door and if we all think carefully for the room we will find the door. If none of us say the words that will stop us looking for the door.'

'It would be better if we remembered there is no door and you can't leave the classroom while the special speaker is speaking in the classroom.'

'On that first day,' Stanley says. 'We all met each other.'

'The seating was assigned,' Drew says. 'Us three were sitting next to each other on the ground because we were on the same ship. Rostered to the same instrument panel.'

'Stanley kept saying, How did we get here? Are they organising us to get home?' Drew says.

'No,' Stanley says. 'I didn't say that.'

'I tried to help,' Alba says. 'I said I didn't know.'

'No,' Stanley says. 'I don't think so. I was happy to be there. They made a beautiful job of the classroom. I got on the ship to France willingly. The letter of credit. What would I know? I am so stupid.'

'Drew didn't say anything,' Alba says. 'She was looking at her phone. She'd tied it around her wrist like it was a watch. Then she started looking around but for a completely different reason. *They really have done a beautiful job with this place?* That's what Drew said, and she was right. They had made a beautiful job of the classroom and the tents around the classroom and then they took Drew's phone watch.'

'I think I said it was nice to meet you,' Stanley says.

'Again,' Drew says.

'Huh?' Alba says.

'Had we not met each other before?' Drew says.

'I am thinking very hard for a moment but trying not to go quiet like we did the last time we tried to think very hard.'

'I remember the truck,' Alba says. 'Getting willingly onto the truck.'

'The ship,' Stanley says. 'To France.'

'That vegan superfood buddha bowl on Mondays was so good,' Stanley says.

'We met each other on the first day,' Drew says. 'On the first day at the classroom. The seating was assigned and we met each other and Stanley said it was nice to meet us. I'm not sure about the phone, but if I had one, I wouldn't have needed it for long because they gave us all new things.'

'Let's agree to disagree,' Stanley says. 'And be quiet enough to hear the noise completely. To hear that it is getting louder. We are tired again. More tired than we are scared, because the ship will be fine. They made a beautiful job of the ship.'

'And the classroom,' Alba says. 'The classroom was beautiful.'

'The story is we would meet there every day, in the morning, early in the morning – clean, in the white linen they gave us. The comfort of it. And sit on the ground all the same distance apart – so there was no distraction. So there was nothing that would confuse us. There was the class in the afternoon – the class on how to make the ship go, and how to be fit for the ship – but in the morning was the talking classes with the special speakers. So we understood our minds, so we could undo ourselves. So we were tuned so we made the right noises for the ship. Everything before the classroom doesn't matter. Today is the day. What is there if not this day?'

'We sat equidistant apart from each other as if there were

chairs and not just the dusty, dry ground and if we wanted it – life on the beautiful ship *Audition* – we needed no distractions. No distractions in the senses and no distractions in the mind. Make the mind clear of all distraction. There were some things we just didn't need. We were stupid, this was one of the stories we needed. We needed to undo the cunning – the cunning is a distraction. The best thing is to be stupid and we are stupid – it is a gift we needed to return to. It is better to be stupid and it is better to not try and work out things. To not work out escape or freedom or thoughts that are of no use. It is better to be grateful and how lucky are we? We needed to undo our scarcity thinking and see what we have – right in front of us and around us. The beautiful classroom, the amazing spacecraft *Audition*. The ability to leave the past and never remember it. To come from nothing. To be purely. Completely here.'

'We don't leave the classroom when the special speaker is speaking.'

'We don't leave the premises.'

'We eat what we are given.'

'We follow the instructions.'

'We live in the now, unconcerned with anything that has come before the classroom.'

'The classroom has doors, but they are all locked during the classes and meals and while we are asleep.'

'Not to keep us in,' Alba says. 'To keep everything out.'

'We have been stuck for a while,' Alba says. 'Time is doing strange things, but we feel like it has been a long time. The present is refracted through the stories from the classroom which we are not telling properly. The real time goes on one second after the other, but the stories make the real time fold and loop and tangle. The stories and the lack of oxygen. The lack of circulation and the painful shapes we are forced into. My face is almost on my chest now. There is a large nerve that runs the length of my back, maybe it goes even further, but it is squashed at several places now and is making me dizzy and I am having trouble breathing. I try to take a deep breath, but it is cut short by the space and I almost choked. I cough and gasp and when I am able to stop coughing you are both still silent and the only sound is the new terrifying noise that seems to signal a new direction. Drew. Drew? Are you awake? Don't be silent asleep. I know you're not asleep, the ship seesaws slightly toward you. Drew, what are we going to do?'

'Shhh.'

'I think,' Alba says, 'we are dying.'

'There's no silence anymore,' Drew says. 'The bang bang of the terrible noise makes sure of it. We were stupid to be quiet and now the terrible noise makes no silence possible – to remind us. We are all holding it in – the tears, the sob. Crying isn't going to help any of us and it will probably really hurt. An uncontrolled sob will force us up and into the ship hard and then who can tell if there would be a ripple of sobs that could batter us up into the corners and possibly break the ship. But now Stanley is overcome. And there is a risk with Stanley overcome that the two of us will be overcome as well. It really does seem inevitable. And with no hope what is left to do? What is it to be stuck like this, with no escape or at least if there is an escape, an escape that is unknown to us?'

'I can see back over my shoulder and out of the skylight and it is dark outside. Very dark and my brain keeps tricking me that something will happen – that someone will come. That, somehow, we will be okay. But you are right, Drew. You are, at least, I want to say, *Drew is always right*. We will die. But our brains still need convincing. That's the problem. The brain wants to survive so it won't help at all in this situation. What's the way out? Would it be better to die now, at our own hands and in our own timeframe? With some control. Or would it be better to go on to the end? No one can tell us. None of us know but we are all thinking it.'

'We covered nothing of any use in the classroom. Looking back now, most of the special speaking was self-improvement. And it improved out of us anything that would be of any use now.'

'Eventually,' Stanley says, 'We can't look back anymore. We can't sit here remembering and stewing over all the perceived slights and the old resentments. Eventually, we have to be here – like, totally here.'

'Like that,' Drew says. 'That is from the classroom and it's completely useless and not the truth at all.'

'What?' Stanley says. 'That thing about not looking back anymore?'

'I don't think I got on the ship to France willingly,' Alba says. 'Can anyone remember who the president was? Or the prime minister? Or what we were eating?'

'Monday,' Drew says. 'Vegan superfood buddha bowl.'

'But can you remember eating a buddha bowl?'

'When I look back before the classroom,' Drew says. 'It looks like a collage. Like someone has taken a whole bunch of separate things and squashed them together.'

'That seems unlikely,' Stanley says.

'But as likely as anything else,' Drew suggests.

'Occam's razor,' Alba says.

'Yeah,' Drew says. 'If we had any fucking clue what the most likely thing was.'

'Fuck knows,' they all say.

'Does anyone know where we are?' Stanley says. 'Like in the scheme of things.'

'We're moving toward something different in the distance,' Alba says. 'Something I can almost feel the pull of. But maybe that's just hope. I wasn't even sure whether to tell you, when I saw it. Hope is the problem. It's like a virus. *What is the point*, I asked myself, *of spreading that?* We are listening, even while I'm talking, and the ship is still making the strange new noise and maybe it's the new thing in the distance that has changed our course so dramatically. But what is the noise? And more importantly, most importantly, does anyone know where we've been?'

'Were we always tall?' Drew asks.

'No,' say Stanley and Alba.

'No,' says Drew.

'I was normal sized,' Drew says. 'For years, like possibly I was slightly shorter than other people.'

'What was your house before the classroom like?' Stanley says.

'Don't you know?' Alba says.

'No,' says Stanley. 'I never went to your house. I've never stepped in your house.'

'Are you sure?' Alba says.

'Well. Yes,' says Stanley. 'For starters, I doubt there would be room for both of us in your house and I am pretty sure we never met before we got big.'

'I'll say it quickly, before I get completely pulled into how great the ship is and how lucky I am, when did you start getting big?' Drew says.

'In the classroom,' Stanley says.

'Not in the classroom,' Drew says. 'We were big when we got to the classroom. Before the classroom.'

'Nothing matters before the classroom so here we go again.'

'When did you start getting bigger?'

'Me?' Stanley and Drew say together.

'Yeah,' Alba says. 'Either. Both.'

'Maybe, like a couple of years ago?' Stanley says. 'I don't sound sure.'

'Tell it like a story,' Drew says. 'Maybe it might be easier, maybe it might stop us from thinking about what we would know and how stupid we are and what a beautiful job they've done with the ship.'

'I was talking to a beautiful woman,' Alba says.

'Once upon a time,' Stanley says.

'Once upon a time,' Alba says. 'Once upon a time I was talking to a beautiful woman at a party, at my house, and my wife – who was also a very beautiful woman – rushed over, put her hand on the top part of my arm and said, *He's leaving. Edward's leaving.* I'd just told him, over the phone from my apartment hundreds of miles away, that I talk to his secretary more than I talk to him. I looked up and away from the first beautiful woman to see Edward, leaving the party I had organised for him – well, my wife had called a caterer. Then I touched the arm of the beautiful woman who was not my wife and said, *Excuse me.* I did not say anything to my wife. I went out to the cars and there he was, Edward, standing next to my Lotus Esprit and asking the valets if it was my car. I said, smiling, trying to joke, *Where're you going?* Edward said, *Can I have the keys to your car?* I asked about, why couldn't he take the limo? But it was blocked in by other cars. I said I didn't think he should drive, that he was a little excited and said, *Don't drive my car*, and tried to sort it out with the men who were looking after all the car keys. But Edward was already in the car. Was he familiar with a stick-shift? Had he driven a stick? Yes. And the car squealed and hopped and it was clear he had not. *Be ginger with it* – and then he was gone and I shouted out from the footpath of a seedy part of Beverly Hills, *Hey baby*, and the guy in the passenger seat of the red convertible yelled out, *How about a freebie it's my birthday.* It wasn't really a question he didn't even slow down. *Dream on*, I shouted back and I made a shaking motion with my hand, not like a wanking sign but anyone watching would think that is what I meant. She said, *It's gonna be really slow tonight.* And I said, *Maybe we should get a pimp, you know? Carlos really digs you.* Or maybe it was, *Maybe we should get a pimp. You know Carlos really digs you?* She was wearing a blonde wig and she was right. *We say when, we say who, we say how much.* She did not look like Carol Channing in the wig. I wasn't sure who Carol Channing was, I said, *No. I love this look.* And I flattened down the blonde bob and told her it was very glamorous. *Glamour choice*, I said. Then there was a screeching and we both turned round. *Oh yo. Oh yo. Catch this.* And she was like, *That's a Lotus Esprit* and I was like, *No. That's rent.* And the Lotus was all over the road and then it slammed into the curb, nose first, butt hanging out into the street. And I was like, *You should go for him. You look hot tonight. Don't take less than a hundred. Call me when you're through, take care of you*, and I pointed at her, gentle, my index finger softly in the skin that was showing in her low-cut dress. She hugged me, *Take care of you*, and as she walked away I said, *Work it, work it baby. Own it.* And she leaned in the car and I could see her talking to him and then she stood up and turned away from the car so he could see the cut out of her tight dress through the passenger window, then he said something, and she turned around and opened the door and they drove off. Still bunny hopping a little because I really don't think he could drive stick.'

'Then what?' Drew asks.

'I think I know,' says Stanley. 'It was Christmas.'

'It was often Christmas,' Drew says. 'I remember Christmas a lot from our life before the classroom.'

'Often,' Stanley says. 'It was Christmas and I was working in the hospital – as a nurse and as the police officer who was called after the train went over the man that fell on the tracks in Chicago and was saved and I was running for my life because we had only meant to steal his wallet we didn't expect the man whose name was Peter to step back and fall on the track and we were running because on the security cameras at the train stop it would definitely look like we pushed him. And I was standing close to the woman who had saved Peter and who had been told only family could follow him into the ward and she said, quietly, *I was going to marry him.* So, I ushered her into the room and I said, *Hey, only family* and I said, *She's his fiancée.* And we hadn't been able to have Christmas because we had come, as a family, to see Peter in the hospital and we met the woman who had saved Peter and was also his fiancée and was also called Lucy and we asked her to our delayed Christmas dinner and Jack was coming, Peter's brother. And she should come and she said she wouldn't. But she did and we heard her say she wasn't really Peter's fiancée and we also tested her because we didn't hear her say she wasn't really Peter's fiancée but we suspected it because we were Peter's brother and he hadn't mentioned anything about a fiancée and we were Peter's fiancée, Ashley Bacon, and we left a message on his phone saying, *I've been thinking and yes, I'll marry you.* And it was snowing. And Christmas. And Vivian said she would leave money for me at the front desk of the fancy hotel where she was staying with Edward but Barney didn't like the look of me so he called up and he told me to wait here and I leaned over and breathed into the mirrored reception desk and an old couple were watching me and I said, loudly, *Fifty bucks, Grandpa. For seventy-five, the wife can watch.* And my mum buys me a whole bunch of really nice clothes – really nice clothes – ropas muy bonitas – and they are all a size too small for me and it's meant to be aspirational and I am the mother and I checked and it's totally achievable – the one size smaller. And then I cry because it is cruel and then the next morning the new maid who doesn't speak English holds up the jacket from the really nice clothes, the jacket I loved and then tried on and it didn't fit and I cried and she says, *Just try it on*, and I say, *It doesn't fit*. And she says, *Just try it on*, over and over and I do and it fits.'

'So you are smaller?' Alba says. 'Overnight you are smaller?'

'Hm,' says Stanley. 'Yeah. I guess this is not the right story. This is a story of getting smaller and we are trying to work out how we got bigger.'

'Correct,' Drew says.

'We are by the pool,' Alba says. 'The snow has stopped and all my clothes fit. There are tables set up around the pool all of them with white tablecloths and silver cutlery and she is in a terracotta culotte suit and a white shirt. I mean, I hardly recognise her, I'm scared to hug her in case I wrinkle her and when we sit down she is framed by a bush of pink and white flowers and the curtains are drawn and the office is dark and we are almost there and Morse is totally going to sign his company away and we will sell it off and make millions and I might be able to buy another Lotus Esprit and then he tells us to leave the room, he wants to talk to Morse and he means me as well and I am raging and then I am in front of her and I slap her hard right across the cheek and I say to her, *You're a hooker. Maybe you're a very good hooker, you know? Maybe if I do you, then I wouldn't care about losing millions of dollars. Because I have to be very honest with you. Right now, Vivian, right now I really do care. I really do. And right now I am really pissed, you know? Right now I am just freaking out. So maybe if I screw you, huh, and take you to the opera, then I could be a happy guy, just like Edward.* And I push her, and I am going to rape her.'

'So, you got big through rape?' Drew says.

'Yeah,' Alba says. 'Yes. When I slapped her I was bigger than Vivian. All the strength of the power of the patriarchy made that slap possible and made me big.'

'Even though you were small?' Drew says.

'Yes,' says Alba. 'When Peter came back it was very apparent how much shorter than Peter I was.'

'Yes,' Stanley says. 'Yes, there were taller people than me all around me. I was one of the smaller people – there were many of us.'

'There were many small people around us – in the halls, in the canteen where I was in a coleslaw-eating competition. It was a very large barrel of coleslaw and I was eating it and I ate it the fastest and there were people everywhere and I ate it the fastest – there were two of us eating – and I won and I spat a mouthful of coleslaw into the air and people were chanting my name. And we were all small, but I was the biggest. I was the adult in the school. I was back – to get a place in the minor league, to get my high school diploma, so I could get a job somewhere other than the luau-themed postal supplies store.'

'Post is dead.'

'Post was dying and I was at high school as a twenty-five-year-old man, and a girl came over to me and said, *I'm sixteen* and I was like, *Damn. Why do they have to be so god-damn beautiful.* I was big then. I was bursting out and I said to her, *You can't do this and respect yourself.* I said, *I would have died for you.* I said, *I live to like you and I can't like you anymore.* I was her turtle. I was her cat.'

'Wrong way,' Alba says.

'I was bursting out,' says Drew.

'I took off my glasses and pulled my hair out of its ponytail,' Stanley says, 'and cut and coloured my hair and made it curlier and made it straighter and I pulled it off my face and took off my oversized coat and put on lipstick and I was bursting out. I was small and then someone took me under their wing and then I became more popular than them and I say to them, *You're a virgin who can't drive* and I save the newly crowned Miss United States' life and I am crowned prom queen and I say *Find out who you are and try not to be afraid of it. Come on Dover move your bloomin' arse* I say a long, long time ago.'

'It was my thirteenth birthday and I wished I was thirty,' Alba says. 'And I'm seventeen again, and in one kiss all my good luck and all his bad luck swaps and I am unlucky and I could hear the voices in the heads of women and I couldn't lie and my angel messes up and I die so I get a free body pass and I end up in the body of an old, white rich guy and I travel back and forward in time.'

'Once I was big we could do anything,' Alba says. 'And we decided to do this.'

'We did many things and we were many places all at once and then we came to the classroom.'

'But how?'

'I realised,' Stanley says. 'And I said to the person we were with, I said, *I have to go*. We ran. I jumped over a trolley of suitcases. The small boy from the elevator led me through the back hallways of the hotel and I stood in the sunroof of a limousine and then I climbed the fire escape even though I was afraid of heights. I hitched up the skirt of my wedding dress.'

'I hitched up the skirt of my wedding dress.'

'I hitched up the skirt of my wedding dress and I ran in my high heels.'

'I ran in my high heels.'

'I ran in my high heels that were flat shoes across the baseball pitch.'

'Across the baseball pitch.'

'Across the baseball pitch through the dark airport in the snow in my leopard skin underwear.'

'I ran in the snow in my underwear through the traffic that was mostly yellow cabs in a New York street along the beach.'

'Along the beach in the rain with my shoes swinging by their sling-backs through an airport, onto a plane.'

'Off a plane and into a taxi and onto another plane.'

'Onto the final plane.'

'And then I was at the classroom.'

'And then I was at the classroom.'

'And then I, also, was at the classroom.'

'We should all lean into the walls that hold us, lean into the sound of the ship, look out, where we can, through the cracks of the skylights at the cold, dark space.'

'Maybe we will die at any minute. Maybe we will die at any minute and then what? Gone. Forever, all this. Gone without a trace. And what is happening on Earth? We are talking but also we are imagining Earth, all carrying on without us, all carrying on without us. Our death, our end, never another one of us, and all the while someone somewhere has room. Who has room?'

'Did you say goodbye to your family?' Stanley says.

'I did not,' Drew says. 'Or maybe, the last time I saw then I said goodbye to them like I would see them next time. Or maybe I didn't. Maybe our relationship had sunk to a level where I didn't even say goodbye. Where maybe . . .'

'I didn't say goodbye,' Alba sounds confident. 'I said, *Fuck off.* I can remember. I decided, *I am big and I am leaving. I thought, I can break them in two. I can do what I want* and I said, *Fuck off* and walked out of the house and up the hill. Running, like this was me finally free, running, the wind, the trees, the mountain and when the truck came I was surprised I was still on a footpath in New York in the airport in the snow. And when the truck came and the people in the truck asked to see my envelope and then said they needed to take me somewhere, I stopped for a moment and looked around, realising what was going on and I thought, I wish I'd said goodbye. Not because I wished I'd said goodbye but because that is what I thought someone in my position should do. Like that was the right thing to do. When faced with this situation, a strange truck and a uniform I hadn't seen before, a request to go, that any decent person would have thought, I wish I'd said goodbye, and I was a decent person, surely, I was decent person.'

'And, *I love you,*' Stanley says. 'And said, *I love you.* I think I also thought that a decent person would wish they had said I love you. But I didn't, not by that stage, not from where I was looking. All I thought was, *Fuck you.* But I sensed, when the truck arrived, that I needed to hide that rage. So, I tried to pick up the envelope beside me – tiny, so tiny I couldn't pick it up – we were so huge – and I fumbled with it and the handcuffs didn't make it any easier and in the end they offered to pick my envelope up for me, with their tiny fingers, and they got my driver's license out of the envelope and they said I needed to go with them and I could have smashed them, like, just one backhander would have floored them, but instead I said, *Okay,* and went with them. Why did I do that?'

'Why did we do that?' the other two echo.

'It seems incredibly out of character,' Stanley says. 'Out

of the character we're describing ourselves to be. It seems so unlikely that we would have done that. That after all that fire, after supporting our best friends, and trying to rape Vivian and being so giant in that high school. After hearing the call and running.'

'The call,' the other two say.

'After feeling so vindicated and so in love. It seems unlikely that the first unmarked truck that came along, the first polite request, we gave up. We fought for nothing.'

'What would we know really though?' Alba says. 'We are so stupid.'

'The terrible noise that is surely signalling a painful and slow death for all of us thumps on and now it's in our bones as it vibrates through the walls of the ship and the ship carries on toward a new odd shape that has caught us.'

'Somewhere, down the hall maybe, some air conditioning turns off and I go to thump on the wall but there is a sudden bang from the noise and the air conditioning is powered back up again. We aren't needed any more. When we started, every now and then we would feel the sag in the ship, only a slight pull nothing disastrous and one of us or, often, more often even, all of us would stop what we were doing and make noise – thump on the wall.'

'Who told you that story?' Alba says.

'Which one?' Stanley says.

'The one about the call and Rufus and the Lotus and the going onto the ship to France willingly?'

'Didn't I tell that story?' Stanley says. 'Like, just now?'

'Yes,' Alba says. 'We all did. But who told you?'

'Torren,' Stanley says.

'Torren,' Drew says.

leaving

The huge ships were lined up in the fields. Ten of them. The first, cities worth of space away from the tenth. The grass around them all was green and high. The teachers had to brush it away from their faces as they ran around the giant crew, making last checks on their suits, which were close fitting and smooth, on the tanks they carried with them like suitcases and, occasionally, picking up anything that dropped from their roll bags. One teacher almost got hit by a T-shirt that fell out of the gap in a roll bag, not quite zipped to the end of its opening. The sun was out. It was a clear day, not a cloud in the sky, it was a blue-sky day and some of the giant crew looked up as they walked along the field. It was a long walk to the ships. The crew were far apart as they walked. They looked over the fields at the crew of the next ship down, some waved. Some tried to shout but it was no good. The grass swept around their knees and the teachers shouted up at them, but it felt like maybe the crew weren't listening. Eighteen giants per huge ship. One hundred and eighty of them were leaving today. Making room for 540 normal-sized humans someone joked. That was the agreed measure because scale was hard. No one really understood how tall they were and whether they'd stopped growing. They'd slowed, thanks to the classroom, the way they kept them slightly sick in the classroom, the food they fed them. Three to one was what everyone agreed – because it made everyone feel more comfortable. The normal-sized, although none of them liked being called that, knew themselves and how tall three of them was – so all of them, the left behind, worked with that.

'I can work with that,' Torren had said, when she went for the job interview. She was running beside one of them now. The giant was strolling but Torren was running, barking up at her, 'Can you check levels on valve nine,' but she wasn't listening.

'Alba!' Torren shouted.

The giant was looking at the sky. They had always been outside – but their view was limited to the roof of the stadium, which the managers sometimes closed completely. The stadium was for them; everything was their size. Which seemed crazy to Torren given how many people her size were there. Torren had talked to her union person about it. They, after all, were the ones doing all the work. The giants were just learning. They were lazy and slow. She called them lazy and slow and giants in her head, but she was careful who she said it out loud to – she needed the job. The giants were pliant, and maybe that's more the word the giants brought to mind. They were slow and just said, *Yes*, a lot. At least the ones that were left did. By the time they got to this stage, Torren's friend Hillary told her. By the time she or Hillary met them, at the classroom, they would be very slow and very, yes, suggestable. Agreeable.

'And you'd want them to be,' Hillary said, 'Have you seen them? They're fucking huge.'

The first time Torren met one of them it was terrifying. They were odd for starters which made her feel terrible, like it was visceral how wrong they looked and the trying not to look was the other thing, the force it took to act normal and polite made her almost faint. Then there was the realisation that they could destroy her. She was average, five-foot-four – she had been since she was twelve, she'd grown fast and then stopped just as fast. She never noticed how short she was until she met someone taller and the giants made her feel like a mouse. Three times as tall. The received wisdom – she'd been working with that before she met them, but it had not prepared her for how tall they actually were. She had three assigned to her at a time and now there were eighteen of them, ambling toward the ship, her and the other teachers face-deep in the long grass, it was just a matter of time before one of the giants stepped on one of them. Torren imagined it, dreamed about it in her sleep, the crush under one of their feet and then the slow confused look, the one they were expert at. Slow and dumb. That was them.

The giants ambled. Torren had noticed it from far away first. There were a couple of them at her daughter's school. Mothers who turned up one day and something was off about them and then they arrived the next day and the next and it became clearer and clearer what was going on. They had trouble getting out of their car, and then they had trouble getting in the classrooms. Their kids were scared of them. Sometimes they wouldn't come out of the school buildings, leaving their mothers hopelessly calling, trying to keep their voices kind but also trying to get the children's attention. 'Marian,' the mother would shout from the door, 'Marian, it really is time to come home now.'

They were ambling now. 'Hurry up,' Torren called. They smiled at her. They always thought she was kind. No matter how horrible she was they smiled at her and said, 'Thank you, kind Torren.' She was sure they wanted to pat her on the head. She was sure of it. That they patronised her because she posed no threat – but they were sedated, heavily. If any of them gave her any trouble she just had to say, *What would you know?* And the trouble one would stop and look confused and settle and nine times out of ten just walk away. But also, there had been nice times – you couldn't live with them and maintain hate for them, especially when you had all the power.

They'd finished early one day, or there had been a problem with something and they hadn't been able to do the day's class and all of them had headed into the sports field to just sort of run about and then when everyone was hot and tired they'd lain down on the barren dusty stadium ground, looking at the sky through the crack in the stadium roof talking to each other. One of them had said, 'I like ice cream', just out of the blue and Torren had said, 'Yeah. Me too.' And the giant had said, 'We should get some ice cream.' And Torren had said, 'What would you know?' And the giant was quiet. Then Hillary had said, 'We should get some ice cream.' She meant to say it just to Torren to test the idea out but the same giant said, 'I like ice cream.' And Torren had looked at Hillary as if, *Look what you've started now* and Hillary looked back like, *We should totally get some ice cream.* And Torren looked around and the giant said, 'I like ice cream.' And Torren said, 'Yes. Stanley. I get it.'

'We should get some ice cream,' the giant said.

'Okay,' said Torren, more to Hillary than to the giant.

Stanley, Hillary and Torren had stood slowly, trying to stay low, under the windows of the storerooms and offices. There was a rung of people above the teachers who got to be inside but not the giants and not the teachers and it wasn't lost on Torren or Hillary. They ran-walked to the warehouse where all the food was kept. The other two giants Torren looked after saw them and ran the same way a few metres behind them.

Torren used her swipe card the whole way. Beeping them in, opening the doors so she could just make sure the coast was clear then waving the others in silently. They finally got to the warehouse. It was huge. They kept all the food there. They walked down the shelves and shelves of dried food which was for the giants, until they came to the very tall refrigerators where they kept the special speakers' food. Hillary and Torren pulled out the first box of ice cream they could find. They sat low beside the refrigerator, hiding behind the large crates, eating ice cream from the boxes. It wasn't meant to be eaten yet. They would put the empty boxes back and at some point, probably, someone would miss out. They ate with Torren-sized spoons made from wood that they found in some noodle packets they fed the teachers on.

'I like noodles,' Drew said.

'Don't fucking try it on,' Hillary said.

Stanley put his huge hand with the tiny spoon into the box to get the ice cream that was right down the bottom and it came out covered, to the wrist, in ice cream. They ate it all. At first Torren suggested eating just a little from a few boxes but when they tried that, they just couldn't stop. Everything was so controlled. The portions of food were particularly controlled – it was all dried powder reconstituted with water but her and Hillary called it ridiculous names: vegan superfood buddha bowl and Greek roasted fish with vegetables – but it was always the same powdered meal replacement devoid of any nutritional value served in massive sipper cups.

Truth be told Torren didn't want to be there any more than the giants would have if they weren't continually told how much they loved being there. It made sense to control what the giants ate. They were astronauts. They needed to get used to space. Once they were gone, they were gone. There'd be no way to adjust for a hungry day. She'd applied for the job because there were no jobs. She hadn't realised what it was about when she applied. She understood all of the words in the job ad separately but had no idea what they meant in the order they were written. She'd seen the giants in her day-to-day and then not seen them as they were steadily taken away, but she never wanted to work with them – no one did. But the ice cream day changed something in her. Stanley's ice cream covered hand. She looked at him now as he walked to the ship, just as he turned his head and smiled and she smiled back.

'You'll miss me,' Stanley said.

Torren laughed and looked out at the ship. It was so far away, why did they have to walk there? 'Probably,' she said. 'Yes, probably.'

'And us,' Alba said, she was pointing her hand between herself and Drew.

Torren shook her head, laughing, but it was true. They were all going and she would miss them. They had been a strange kind of team. Torren had supervision on Fridays and she was always told not to get too close. But she'd broken plenty of rules, they had shirked and stolen and fucked about but now, it didn't matter at all. They'd made it, they were safe enough to leave, she'd taught them well and they were leaving. It probably had very little to do with her, she didn't do any of the important stuff. She just ran them though the drills. The real stuff was done in the morning, in the talking classes. That was where the willingness came from. Torren just trained their bodies to push the switches and pull the levers and read the meters.

They weren't friends. Torren realised that the first week she worked there. She was a handler and they were the captives. But it could look like a friendship. Especially when they were told the things they were told during the talking classes in the dawn light sitting in the area they called the classroom which was really just a corner of the sports field which was trampled and barren and dusty now. There was a stage where the people who stayed inside, the special speakers, would stand and talk and talk and talk. The giants were told they were friends, so Torren needed to say she would miss them now. She needed to tell them she'd miss them as they walked toward the ship

– to make the talking true, to keep everything under control. But really, would she? It would be good to see them go. They were dangerous and annoying, they took up way too much space. It would be good to get everything back to normal and really, and her supervisor had explained this to her, Torren's real job was to make them feel like they were loved. Like they would be missed. Like there were people around who loved them and cared what happened. When she'd told him about the ice cream incident her supervisor had said, 'Good.' She'd thought she would lose her job but he just said, 'Good.' And wrote something in her file.

'What flavour was it?' he asked.

'Vanilla,' she said.

'Right,' he said, and wrote it down. He caught her trying to see what he was writing and said, 'It's just so we replace the box. You don't want anyone missing out on dessert. That wouldn't do.'

Torren left the meeting confused and for the next week or so explored the boundary of just how friendly she was supposed to be with her giants. She started by making the occasional joke. 'That'll keep you going,' she said, as one of the giants carried over a box full of supplies. 'Woah. Fashion,' she said as she finished showing another giant how to put an external spacewalk suit on. Each time she'd check the other teachers' faces and reactions and then push a little bit harder.

'Where are you from?' she said one day to Alba. Alba looked at her, suspicion all over her face spreading through her body. 'Before here.'

'Before the classroom?' Alba said.

'Yeah?'

'Around?' Alba said.

Torren checked the other teachers. They had heard, they

must have, but they carried on, holding guide ropes and pointing at screens from beside where the giants sat.

'Kids?' Torren said.

'Do I?' Alba said. It was a dumb joke – the giants made some terrible jokes. But Torren realised she'd hit a boundary she hadn't expected. They were supposed to be compliant, but Alba was not going to tell her anything. Alba looked at her and Torren could see she was also testing things. Torren could have made her answer the question. 'It would be better if you answered me.' It would be better if you cleaned that up, it would be better if you left. You usually used it in conjunction with the line, 'What would you know?' Which was some kind of stand down command as well. If things got heated because things definitely got heated. She could say it now. 'What would you know? It would be better if you let me know if you had any kids.' Alba was still standing, still looking at Torren.

She was pissing Torren off so she looked around faking surprise and said, 'He's a kid. He has a whole hotel to play with.' It was the first thing that came into her head, it was *Maid in Manhattan*.

Alba just looked at her silently – not looking so dumb. Then Torren said, 'What happened before the classroom doesn't matter so what would you know?' And Alba's face softened and she said, 'Yeah, what would we know?' And went back to what she was doing.

But, the next day at lunch Alba, Stanley and Drew came and sat with Torren – they ate on the ground, they slept on the ground, it was another thing Torren talked to the union rep about. The teachers were always outside with the giants. Usually it was segregated – not by any decree it just worked its way out that way. When they were training like this, all day, a variety of sizes, they ate outside mixed into groups of teachers and groups of giants. Torren had been eating some boiled eggs out of a plastic container thinking about something else, and she'd caught Alba's eye accidentally as she looked out over everyone. And for a minute it looked like Alba had been waiting for that to happen – willing it – and when their eyes did meet she got up and then signalled almost imperceptibly to the others who also got up. Torren rolled her eyes but they didn't get the hint, they never got the hint and they ambled over, sipper cups in hand, casually at their sides, and sat near to her. Torren looked at the sky, she couldn't remember the last time it rained during the day. They sat together in silence eating. Then Stanley laughed.

'What?' Torren said.

'I was just thinking about Alba's kid.' He delivered the lines, there was nothing natural about the way he said it.

'Oh yeah,' Torren laughed – they were so ridiculous and now she had to work in her lunch break so fuck them. 'That hotel you worked in was big, eh?'

Alba, Drew and Stanley nodded.

'And that white pantsuit you tried on.' Torren laughed because surely they would recognise what she was doing, surely they knew Jennifer Lopez, but when she looked up from her lunch the giants were looking at her intently. It frightened her.

'What would you know?' she said and the intensity partially left their faces. 'It would be better if you didn't ask about your job as a maid in the hotel in Manhattan. Nothing matters that happened before the classroom.'

'The food is so good here,' Stanley said.

'Yeah,' Torren said.

'Monday is vegan superfood buddha bowl,' Drew said.

'Yeah,' Torren looked at the sky. 'It's such a nice day, eh?'

'Yeah,' Alba said. 'They really have done a beautiful job with the weather.'

Then Drew said, 'You are so kind to us Torren.'

And it all seemed okay and Torren wasn't sure what she'd been worried about and all the fear she'd had turned to pride at how she could control these huge, dumb things. And after that, every time things got a bit boring for her or a special speaker yelled or told her she wasn't doing something right, Torren would tell the giants another story about how before they came to the classroom they lived in a romantic comedy she liked. And then when it looked like it was getting out of hand she'd just say, 'It would be better if you remembered that everything that happened before the classroom doesn't matter so what would you know?' It passed the time and Torren loved the way they paid attention to her when she told them about *Pretty Woman* or *Spanglish* or *You've Got Mail.*

Stanley had stopped walking – bent down to fiddle with something on his boot.

'Hurry up,' Torren said. She had a timer on her wrist, the launch wasn't going to wait for anyone. This was a lie; in reality there was no rush. They wouldn't leave without them. Not today, not tomorrow. They would wait for them.

Stanley stood up and he was laughing. They were funny, that was the thing Torren had found hard. They were slow and dumb but it was hard to fully write off someone as funny as Stanley. He had a lightness to him. He was one of the funniest people Torren had ever met. There was a warmth to him. Now Alba had broken rank, was coming toward the laughing Stanley, she put her arm round him casually, easily and now they both laughed. One of the other teachers was shouting at Alba now, waving their hands a bit. But Alba ignored her. Torren looked behind herself and as expected she saw Drew, never far behind. Once they found where the ice cream was, Stanley, Alba and Drew returned over and over. Sometimes Torren would find them and they weren't even eating the ice cream but were just hiding behind the boxes by the refrigerators talking to each other. Torren would have to *What would you know?* them because they weren't supposed to be alone together.

Drew ran past Torren – it was still terrifying. She joined the hug with Alba and Stanley and the three of them took off at a run like that, joined and laughing. Torren's earpiece erupted in a chorus of panic. 'It's okay,' she said into it, she'd be in trouble but surely they could have just this. Torren ran up to catch them.

'Come on,' Torren said, running beside them at a sprint while they loped.

'Oh,' Stanley said. 'Yup. Totes.' And the three of them unfolded themselves from the embrace, stopped laughing and started to walk again. 'Runaway moment,' Stanley said and Alba and Drew laughed again. But then they all fell silent, their faces falling into sad seriousness. Torren had convinced herself they wanted to go. But now as the ship got bigger and bigger, the closer they got, she could see they didn't. They were the unwanted. That was clear to them, perhaps it had been from the start. They took up too much room.

Torren looked around and muted her headpiece. 'What would you know?' she said. 'It would be better if you were excited about this and happy.'

The ship was called *The University of Whispers*, but everyone called it *Audition*. From above it had three wings. Like a capital letter 'Y' but what they could see now, as they walked through the tall grass, was the main entry, the docking bay. It was smooth and shiny and painted pink, all of it. Like a white mouse before it gets its fur. Realistically it could be any shape. Once it was out of Earth's atmosphere it would travel in the direction it was pointed. It had been finely tuned. In most buildings they spent money and time making sure noise didn't travel, walls didn't echo. But *Audition* would be the noisiest ship ever built. They'd had exercises but everyone knew it was going to be louder than anything they'd experienced in training. But once they were gone what could the giants do?

Torren looked back behind them at the blue, clear sky. It was so hard to believe how dark it would be once they broke free. It seemed like it should be brighter. Like they should break out into the brightest light. That it would shine and glow, but Torren knew it was dark. She'd wanted to go. Not in *Audition*, not on this trip. But she'd wanted to go when she was a kid. There was a bit of talk about that on the radio, in the air. Why did the freaks get to go? What was it to them? What about all the good citizens who didn't get giant, who just did their work? Worked hard, looked after their family. Did what they were told, were quiet. Didn't they deserve the trip more than the giants? It seemed almost like a prize. A reward, someone said, and that was it, someone else small, normal-sized, said, a reward. They were being rewarded for bad behaviour – for being a threat to everybody else. It was unfair. So, some normal-sized people got together to try and make it as clear as possible just how unfair it was. They wrote messages of complaint to people in power but it was in the conversations that it was at its most powerful. On the streets and buses and trains and on YouTube and on TikTok and on the radio. And maybe Torren had felt the same. Maybe she had said the same things to her friends maybe she had said it felt like a reward. Maybe she had said it doesn't seem fair and what about her, what about her Physics degree and how hard she worked for that? Why couldn't she get a job as an astronaut? And then she lost her job as a part-time physics tutor and there were no other jobs and she was even more angry. But now, from inside, she was very quiet. She'd been quiet from the minute she started her job. The minute she walked inside the stadium. The minute she started walking around towered all about by the giants. Once she saw the looks on their faces.

No one knew for sure, but everyone was sure they were preparing them for something awful. Something terrible. Alba had asked her one night. They'd all been lying outside. They were supposed to be asleep but the night was clear, really Torren couldn't remember a bad day, no rain, no wind stronger than a gentle breeze. It was hot and none of them could sleep and someone said something about going for a walk. They'd dared each other. 'We should,' they said to each other one by one, waiting for someone to stand up. Then it was Alba. Not that she was a leader just that she wanted to and realised there was no point and nothing to lose. Alba wrapping a blanket round her shoulders stood up, so much taller than Torren who slept with them so they could start work early each day. Her supervisor asked about what they did at night and Torren told him, always, that nothing ever happened. 'They just go to sleep,' she said but really it was often like this, awake, looking at the sky – wandering about sometimes.

They could have walked over the fences that blocked the entrances to the stadium. Knocked them down in a single push. One time Drew took a door off its hinges and she wasn't even the strongest of them. They could break out, but they never did. All that stood between it happening was Torren deciding not to say, 'What would you know?' But she would always say it – she needed the job and really she hated them.

Alba, with her blanket round her shoulders not for warmth but as some kind of strange and useless disguise, looking at the sky, walked toward where Torren was lying. All of them quietly mumbling to each other and then Alba, still looking at the sky, asked, clearly but quietly, so only Torren could hear, 'Do you know anything?' and then when Torren shrugged, 'How bad will it be?' And Torren said, 'What would you know? It would be better if you didn't ask questions.' And Alba went back to her ground sheet and lay down and the others were soon quiet and all of them were asleep. When the sun came up the next day, they woke up and went to get food and Torren told them to go to the talking class and they did and they listened and nodded and spoke when they should have and chanted and clapped on cue.

Torren tried to feel it like they were feeling it. They were walking slower than they could that was for sure. She watched them, the three of them, the three she was taking. There were hundreds of others, but these were the three she was responsible for – three of them equals one of her. She watched them. Looking about. Trying to get some kind of sense of the place to take with them. She tried to feel it. This goodbye. They weren't telling them much but they were definitely not telling them that they weren't coming home. Alba kept looking behind her, like she expected to see the past. Like she had a hope that maybe it had been some kind of mistake, that maybe she wasn't that tall. That maybe she had stayed the same size, that she was just going back to work, on the bus, complaining about the way the giants were being rewarded. But then she would look down at the ground, so far away, and realise they were right and there was no hiding it. She was going and not coming back. So, she looked up, to remember the sky maybe. The irony was painful. She'd have all the sky she wanted once she was up there but for now she wanted to try and feel the sky so she could remember it. But then Torren saw, it wasn't the sky, it was the walking under sky. That would not be available to them anymore. They were flying away, up into it.

Torren looked over at the TV cameras. Some of the other teachers had their phones out. Sometimes a giant would smile at the camera, pass a comment like, 'It's very exciting.' Or do something with their hands to show they knew they were on a livestream. A peace sign or a small V with their thumb and forefinger crossed, where an imaginary heart could nestle.

'Won't you tell my family I love them,' Alba said quietly, so quietly so only Torren could hear.

Torren didn't have a clue about Alba's family.

'Make sure my son keeps working hard at school and Kit stays safe and my cat is fed and Rufus gets a walk.'

Torren hadn't realised Alba could speak so quietly.

'What would you know?' Torren said.

'I can't even remember them,' Alba said.

'Nothing that happened before the classroom matters. It would be better if you didn't ask questions about your family.'

'I'll miss you,' Alba said. 'You have been very kind to us.'

'Yeah,' said Torren. 'I'll miss you. Look at the ship,' she said loud enough so Stanley and Drew could hear her. 'Haven't they done a beautiful job of the ship?'

And she watched smiles break on all their faces.

They were at *Audition* now. There was a ramp. One of the first ships was taking off. The wind from its slipstream blew at them and they turned to look, watching it rise, craning their necks, shading the sun from their eyes until it was gone. From below the ships were also Y shaped. From underneath you could see the three wings lifted seamlessly up into the air, up into the sky. There were ten others to launch before *Audition* and then another seven. The first ten were in full flux now. Taking off minutes apart.

'They need to get in,' someone said in Torren's earpiece.

'You need to get in,' she shouted at Stanley and Alba and Drew and they all started walking with purpose, up the ramp. Torren couldn't follow them and not one of them said goodbye and not one of them said thank you and not one of them turned to wave. They were the ship's now and maybe they had forgotten Torren already and she had three new giants waiting to be taught. But Torren waved. As the door moved into place she waved them goodbye and an old phrase came back to her, 'God speed.' But speed was the last thing they needed now. If only they could have had slightly longer on the ground. If only they could have stayed safe here for slightly longer. 'God slow,' Torren thought. 'God slow.' But as the doors closed the roar from inside was so great. She knew they were on their way. That they were gone now. That to them, it was her who was gone. But she stood there and waved.

Alba could see the reflection of Torren waving in the glass in front of them as they walked into the ship. She could have turned. The doors closed, slowly, and she could have waved at Torren but if she turned it would be to look at the sky and she didn't want Torren misunderstanding. Fuck Torren. She was watching the reflection of the blue of the sky disappear as the door shut. The ramp of the ship raised so the scene disappeared from the bottom and the sky – she bent her knees slightly – the sky was the last to go. She stepped back slightly, toward the door that was all but completely shut.

'Wrong way,' Drew said. She was caring for her really, knew the pain of it, better than anyone. Knew the way the heart was wrenched out of the body, out of the current situation, up into the sky. High. They were about to follow the heart but they needed all of their body in the ship. 'Come on,' Drew said but not until the door was completely shut and both of them were crying, for the first time. For the first time as giants. They had been full of the growth. Full of the strength and then they had been full of the hate and then even that had abandoned them. From the day they'd walked into the classroom, they knew they were done. There was no place for them. Not anymore. There was no space for them – no room. The surrender had come over them rapidly, like possibly in the moment, in the moment the doors of the stadium closed behind them. Possibly that moment, when they were at their most sure, storming. Storming away. That was it. They were a storm and then they were the calmest blue sky and the calmest sea and a lake with no swell whatsoever. But the storm was the last thing. The first thing. There was nothing before the storm, before the doors of the stadium – nothing mattered before the classroom. They had come willingly to the classroom. None of them could remember – a special speaker had told them about it, how they came willingly, but none of them could remember it and that's why Drew waited, that's why Alba watched the reflection until it was gone. They'd missed the last time they left, they didn't want to miss this one. They were nothing if not teachable. If they'd paid more attention to what they were leaving when they were taken to the classroom maybe the storm wouldn't have left so easily. She wasn't going to miss this departure.

'If we were smart,' Stanley said, as he lugged his heavy equipment case up on to the control panel in front of his chair. 'We'd just say goodbye to that,' he waved his hand at the door, 'and hello to all this,' and he waved at the roof of the ship. Then he laughed, hard. 'But we're stupid.'

The roof above his station where the lights were warming into some kind of natural glow was high and there was plenty of room. The light was a blue colour, but it had a warmth to it as well. None of them had noticed it before because they had only been in a simulator and, they realised now, the simulator was not a perfect match for the ship. Generally, in the simulator they could see some natural light. Coming up under the door of the room, or through the places the walls didn't perfectly meet. None of them had taken the time to stop and think about what it was going to be like to be here, for real. But they saw it now. There was a slight panic in them. Stanley looked up and then at his arm, the one that had been carrying the case. He looked at the light on his hand, which was un-gloved now. The way the blue played on his tattooed skin. The blue of his veins shifting in between the hard blue-black lines. Alba could see he was mulling it over, whether or not to mention it.

'Goodbye,' Drew said. Waving at the door. 'Hello,' waving at the ceiling.

'Yeah,' Stanley started pulling things out of his equipment case now, then more quietly, 'Yeah.'

The three of them set up in silence. But the bridge was noisy. Beside them, arranged in a Y-shape that mimicked the whole ship, were five other sets of threes sitting at identical control panels, chattering about this and that. Some of them were laughing, some much more serious. Alba, Stanley and Drew worked together quietly to set up their control desk. They had been assigned to Torren on the first day – the other threes had been assigned their own teachers. On that first day, Drew exchanged a look with Alba, like they might do something, make some trouble, but they didn't know each other from Adam so it was a wasted and useless act of rebellion. Now wasn't the time and maybe it would never be the time. But Alba returned the look out of habit perhaps. Out of hope. As if it meant something, as if it could mean something, but it meant nothing. Just a look. Just a look exchanged.

It had been by chance. All the groups were pulled out of hats. Alba didn't see them pull anyone's name out of a hat but that's what they told them had happened. This should have been a sign. No one had been asked to submit a CV but maybe they already knew everything they needed to about them. Maybe somewhere there was a big database, but how? All their information shared somehow. Alba was unsure of how they even knew who had grown. Sometimes she thought that maybe they just patrolled the streets watching for them as they left their houses but no one could remember their houses or leaving them or walking in the streets. They would have been easy to find – like flushing a rabbit warren out with a ferret. But then she remembered the envelope of forms they'd handed her. How it had her name at the top and her address and, now that she thought about it, two other signatures with names redacted and the word 'family' in brackets next to the thick black line. So, maybe they hadn't been patrolling the streets. She'd never really thought it through much further than this. She lost interest and found herself thinking really it would be better if she did something else and nothing before the classroom really mattered at all.

The control panels were the same as the ones in the simulator, but they seemed somehow heavier. Alba was looking around at the others as she unpacked the things from her case. She hadn't met any of the other threes, didn't know them. Why hadn't she talked to them? She'd seen them in the classroom in the special speaker classes. She knew her place. She looked around as they sat at their seats. They all knew their place. They'd been taught in threes, and they sat in their threes in the morning talking classes and now here they were – all of them. None of them had been told how many there would be. They'd worked in threes and now here they were eighteen of them. None of them looked shocked.

They were all just taking out their things, the comms headset, the lead for the headset, the watch they put on their wrists that monitored them and sent information back. She looked at it, she assumed it sent information back, that it was a way to make sure they were okay, but, she looked up again and around all of them, trying not to be noticed. A water bottle. It was full at the moment but where did you fill it up again. Alba looked around and then she caught Stanley also looking around and she couldn't be sure but as they looked away from each other – fast – Alba wondered if they were both looking for the same thing. They'd been told there was a change of clothes in the cabins where they slept. They hadn't seen their cabin yet, none of them had. Now was not the time for looking at their cabin, now was the time for work. Now was the time for take-off. Had there really been nothing they could have done? It seemed like it just wasn't worth thinking about it, what would she know anyway?

There was a flash then, in Alba's mind. That bright moment of freedom. Striding. Rage fuelling her arms and legs. The way she moved with such balance, like a cup fitting into a saucer. Like she had always been meant to stride like that. Away. She thought around the image and she was pretty sure in this imagined moment she had been completely happy. She stood, and in the privacy of her body felt it throughout her – leaving with very little thought of coming back.

The control panel in front of her lit up. Not for the first time she wondered if maybe the lights and the buttons and the processes were all fake. Just there so they felt like they had something to do. So they felt implicated or rather, involved, and that, really, maybe everything was being controlled from somewhere else. She looked out to where in any other vehicle a window would have been but the blast shields were up and she couldn't see a thing of the field, or the stadium they'd walked from. Some of the crew were already revolting. Some had their feet on the control panels and were leaning back in their seats talking to others of them. Talking like it was so good to be free of that bullshit. She watched them. Soon there was a voice in their ears. All of their ears saying, *It would be better if you all worked hard and did what you've been told to do* and Alba stopped thinking about the window and the leaving and just started working and so did everyone else. Feet came off counters and the noise of chatter and laughter went out of the room.

Feet came off counters and the noise of chatter and laughter went out of the room. The voices wouldn't come forever, Stanley thought as he ran through a checklist. Why did they need so many identical control panels? Each with three people. Each with the same functions. Stanley didn't know much but he knew the voices in their earpieces couldn't last all the way to where they were going. Time didn't work like that. Space didn't work like that and sound was only waves and he was sure they wouldn't be able to talk to them all the way, and then what? The control panel was noisier here. Noisier than in the simulators. He wound a dial and the static crack was louder. The checklist said it had to go to twelve but by seven he could hardly manage it. The others in the room were trying theirs as well and the room was almost unbearable. The sound went through him. He could feel it in his skin. It was much louder and more unpleasant than it had been in the simulator. He tried each of the channels but no one from the control tower was listening. He asked over and over if someone could talk to him but no one would. Other crews were asking too. Into the headsets, yes, but also each other. As if any of them would know. There was no point in questions about the sound. He looked at the door but the door was shut now, but not shut enough for him to be trapped, surely. He reached for a dream he'd had. The way it felt. That was truly what all this was about, he was sure of it. The way it had felt to leave. The balance in his step, how good it felt to leave, to run up that hill, the way his stride just moved him ever forward.

The noise was so uncomfortable. It went through him. Everyone was starting to complain about it now, putting their hands up to their ears, trying to make it stop but it carried on. A message came over their headsets or maybe it was outside, amplified through the speakers on the wall, *What would you know? It would be better for everyone if you just did your work.* And then gradually several of them put their hands down, taken by some light that needed their attention on the control panel and then Stanley found himself touching another control turning the dial up to twelve and the noise was still there and it still hurt but there was nothing he could do. He saw that now. As it left, the fight in him, as it slowly seeped out of him, he thought for a moment of all the things he could do but then when he went back all these ideas were gone and there was nothing to do but carry on. And he carried on, because any other idea was gone. And like all the other times it had happened he tried to hold onto the idea, right at the end, right as it left, right at that very last moment he tried to count it, count all the power he had in him. All the power in his arms. His bigness. The way they were all so much bigger than any of the people that pushed them around, tried to hold onto that last minute where he remembered that all he had to do was turn around and say, *Let's not do this.* And then, it was gone and all that was left was the certainty that really, he knew nothing and was stupid and it would be better if he did his work. It was like walking into a room having forgotten what it was you went in there for, and it was all, *The work*, then, *the light, the light*. All the controls needed their attention now. And then he remembered, for a while they had all wondered if the controls were only there so they had something to do. That really the ship was controlled from outside the ship. Like the months of training were only there to train them better into being compliant. All of it was just to get them on the ship. The beautiful spacecraft *Audition*. They had made a beautiful job of the ship. How lucky they all were – him, Drew, Alba – to be in the magnificent spacecraft *Audition*.

They couldn't talk to them all the way.

The thought came to Drew as another message came over the headsets. It was just logistical, just an item on a checklist. They couldn't talk to them all the way. Drew didn't know much but she knew they couldn't talk to them all the way. That eventually there would be a lag. She looked around, but maybe they would be dead before that happened. Maybe they would all be dead. This logic played with her a bit, it seemed to defy logic. It would have been easier to kill them all on Earth and then shoot them into space – you needed so little for that. You needed nothing – no life support, no gravity, no sleeping areas, or uniforms or anything like that. Why would they do it this way? They'd been at the classroom for months. She was sure of it. They'd been quite smart when they came in. But eventually they had trouble remembering how gravity worked. Had trouble walking through doors. All their senses about trajectories and the way space worked left them and they found themselves clumsy by it and slow. It happened to them all. It was like some fundamental understanding of the world had gone and it was making the world hard for them to navigate. The teachers spent hours talking to them. There was never any silence. No quiet at all. Stanley, Alba and her sometimes talked about things. They'd hide behind the boxes beside the refrigerators and talk about this place and the place they came from and where they might be going. But then Torren would find them and say it would be better if they forgot about all that and got back to training. The sound of the static got louder again. It was terrible and she suspected this was what it would be like the whole way without the dulling of the stupid words the teachers spoke to them. None of them were captains. They were all exactly the same. It was perhaps a redundancy. Many of them would have to go before the ship was in trouble. It seemed logical. Which made her think, maybe, she'd been wrong, maybe it was what it looked like. A journey rather than an execution. What would she know though? They were all so stupid.

They spent all morning sitting together, hundreds of them, in the classroom listening and listening and listening to what seemed like lies to start with but became more and more realistic as the hours went on. In the late afternoons the teachers took them to the simulators. Sometimes her mind would drift and she'd wonder about the people she knew before the classroom. But fuck those fuckers. They were better off without her and this made her boil. Fuck them. They were having fun. She was sure of it. They would have their precious rooms in nice hotels and apartments with cats and Rufus was probably there and the prom. She wasn't in the way anymore. Maybe she had a job before – in the ticket booth of the Chicago trains, in a book shop, on a street corner – but she was easily replaced. Maybe that was what they'd been trying to tell them all – that they were easily replaced. That really this was the only place they were needed at the moment. Right here. Torren was probably the worst of them. Then she remembered part of a whispered conversation with Alba and Stanley. *Pretend to be friends with her.* They had no hope of escape, none of them maybe even wanted to escape but they liked the idea of the ice cream and of knowing perhaps a little bit what was going on in the next bit so they laughed with Torren and smiled and maybe Drew flirted with her a bit, just a bit. But fuck her. She was going back to the classroom now – maybe she had some leave – and they were here. They were here in final checks. She didn't want to go but what she wanted felt broken. She searched her body for it, the desire for anything, but it was all gone. She was passive and broken and then there was the switch to switch. The Perspex cover to lift and then the lever to pull down. They all looked at each other so they all did it at the same time. Time didn't work like that she told herself. They all looked at the one next to them and that meant that someone would pull the first lever which meant the last lever would be God knows how many seconds behind the first and it made her think again that there was nothing under the lever that the lever went nowhere. And something rose up in her for a minute and she thought, *It would better if I just pulled the fucking lever.* And there it was. They didn't need to tell them all the way because they had told them enough times that they told themselves now. 'Fuck,' Drew said to herself. 'Fuck.'

'Fuck,' Alba said to herself. Drew was swearing at herself and so was Stanley – she caught them in the corner of her ear. Stanley's face was pulling in odd ways and his eyes were checking to make sure no one was noticing. They were unreliable because Alba and Drew noticed because they were also looking round to make sure no one heard them. You could sort of feel the rage coming off him. Alba could anyway. They had spent a lot of time together. Alba looked from Stanley to Drew. Stanley was the angriest. It didn't always look like that because when he thought anyone was looking he smiled but sometimes just with his mouth. He was often fighting against something strong inside. To start, when anyone normal sized talked to him he'd smile with his eyes, but as the talking at him went on, the light in his eyes would fade and the rage would start to show through. But he would keep nodding and smiling his fake smile. For a moment, back when they first arrived, Alba thought maybe Stanley was their only hope. If anyone could save them it would be Stanley. If anyone could save them. If anyone would hold on it would be Stanley. Every time they were asked to do the next terrible thing, Alba would look at Stanley in the hope. In the dream that he would say something, but it was always the same, the smile, the grinning mouth and the raging eyes. And now he was swearing at himself. Beautiful Stanley and his mumbling.

Alba had seen it before, plenty of times. Sometimes she'd wish Stanley would swear at the person in front of him but there was no telling him to do that. None at all. They were all keeping their heads down, they were all working hard. Trying not to get broken as fast as they were. Trying to be there. Alba really didn't know – what would she know? It was a terrible situation they found themselves in. A terrible situation. There was no way out of it. And the teachers were kind to them, they were all so stupid and they had made a beautiful job of the ship. A few weeks in Alba had sat down. Just sat down in the hope they might just leave her but they were soon on her. Telling her to get up. Telling her it was all right. Telling her she could have ten minutes. 'And then what?' she'd said. And they'd said,

'What would you know? It would be better if you just got up after ten minutes.' And she knew she was sunk. Whether they had put it in them early on, when they first started growing or whether it was a new thing, something they did when they got to the classroom. It was all pointless. Everything was pointless, so she just got up again immediately and went back to what she was doing. Not waiting the ten minutes was her only course of revolt. So she stood up immediately and went back to pushing a button directly after Drew pushed the button beside her. It was the worst. And they were here now. The checklist was almost complete. None of them wanted to go. She looked around. You'd think in a room full of this many people someone would be excited, but none of them were. They were all just going through the motions. Their lives were over. The blast screens came down now, so they could see the field again and the stadium a long way in the distance. There wasn't a soul anywhere in their eyeline – all the people on the ground were tiny compared to them. All the people were gone. All the other people. The other ships were too far away and the one beside them was taking off. The noise was palpable now. It was louder than ever. They'd been taught to say 'problematic'. This painful feeling is problematic – this broken bone, this open wound. And then someone said, someone at one of the other desks, 'I just don't think I can handle it anymore.' And someone next to them said, 'What would we know though? It would be better if you were able to handle it. It would be better if all of us could just handle it.' And Alba heard it and felt herself slipping and tried to hold on to not handling the noise, just holding tight, just being in the discomfort and the caring, really deeply, about how terrible the noise was and then she was handling it and there was no way back. No way at all. No way at all.

She looked at the others, there was no way of talking about

it to anyone because it was gone now. They all looked the same. All the uniforms were the same. All their hair was short now, shaved. None of them were wearing make-up and even though they were all different – like their bodies – they all looked the same. There were waves and waves of them leaving in other ships. And she started to think, started to remember when she had looked different. When she had started growing and for the first time she remembered that she'd worked in a laundry. And her job was to wash and iron and fold. She looked down, in her mind's eye, at her small hands, she looked down at the way her hand used to look wet in a tub of warm soapy water and the way it looked pulling large sheets from a huge dryer and then as time passed, maybe a day, maybe a year, opening the door of a washing machine. Maybe her hands were smaller than average and sometimes people would yell and she would remain polite because she was good at that. She was unremarkable.

'Alba?' Drew was talking to her. Had been talking to her. Any minute now the sound would be hard again. 'Can you give me that reading?'

Alba looked at the dial and read the number off.

'Right,' said Drew.

'You have to concentrate,' Stanley said.

'Do I though?' Alba said. Gesturing toward the control panel. 'Like, do we?'

'Well,' Stanley laughed slightly. 'It'd be better if we did.' And then for a split second looked disgusted at himself and then took up laughing again. They were their own worst enemies now. All of it had probably just been for this. Alba looked around. Something told her that soon she wouldn't notice it. That soon none of them would notice it. They would be wrong if they noticed. It was better if they just didn't notice.

'Yeah,' Alba said. 'Yeah.'

on the edge of the gates of hell at the end of space and time

‘Torren told us,’ Alba says, and the ship lurches hard and then shakes at itself. The strange new noise freed somehow and now louder and more confident. The new noise that is the old noise, the first noise, the one they brought from Earth, the one hidden to them because it would be better if they lived with it, but always there, grating, chewing at them. The noise that really keeps the ship going bare now. Out in the open, now they are questioning everything.

Alba looks behind herself again. She can see their new destination. Bright in the dark. Orange.

‘It’s like a ring,’ she says. ‘A ring of orange.’

‘That sounds familiar,’ Stanley says.

Another lurch and then a drop and new noises. Screws loosening. Panels under stress.

‘It’s like hitting turbulence in a plane,’ Drew says. None of them had been in a plane. ‘Like the-air-hostesses-are-all-buckled-in level turbulence.’

It is that bad and then stops. Maybe there’s a gravitational pull that they’ve fallen into. Maybe not. Maybe they’ve crashed into something. It becomes very clear then, to all of them all at once. The past is confusing, none of them are sure of the past, but the present is here and falling in on them. There is no confusion in the present because death is sharpening their minds. Death sharpens everything acutely into the present moment and it feels like the truth. As if everything had been a lie before this one moment. They have been wrong about everything. And now, here they are.

Bang, the ship heaves again.

It is quite possible they will die not knowing. It's completely possible they will die and have no idea how they got here and what came before they got to the classroom. And somewhere, light years from where they are, in a drawer perhaps there is a file and that drawer is in a filing cabinet and it tells the whole story. But they won't know. It's all confusing. Where they started and where the stories ended. But in the moment, as their heads smash this way and then that. That pain. That pain is truth. There is truth in pain. And then it's gone. The initial hit, the pain dulls and rings or settles in, but the truth is gone.

'Are we going to die?' Stanley says. Always talking. Always talking. And then the sound comes worse than the physical pain, because it can soothe them or it can harm them and it harms them very hard and that is that. The sound which had been their fuel and their invisible friend turns on them in the ship. Even when they all stopped talking it was there, but they hadn't been able to hear it again until now. They'd heard it once on the ground and it had been the bed of the whole trip without them noticing because even at their loudest they were never enough. The hum that was magnified – the hum and the hiss of the station not quite on the station, of the vibrations of the microphone. That hum raises itself now and that is pain.

'What about when we first took off?' Stanley says. They had to shout at each other now, over the noise. The tone sets their teeth on fire if they hit certain places in their mouths, like if their teeth touch each other in the forming of an 's' their whole face is set alight. But still they talk over each other. Shout, even though the shouting made the fire worse.

'In the beginning.' This is also a way that stories started.

'But surely, we don't want to go right back to the beginning?'

'Where do you want to start from?'

'I was just thinking – well, I think we're all thinking it really – but I was thinking if we can go back to when it was working. Like properly, maybe we can backwards engineer it back into working again?'

It occurs to them now, suddenly and fully, what they'd done. That although they were useless, the sound was also useless without them – unable to deliver all the tones the ship needed. The power there had been in their silent rebellion. They had completely and permanently broken the ship and set themselves growing again. The growing, this growing was some kind of symptom of success rather than failure.

'Maybe we were right to stop talking?' Stanley says.

And they all think back and they see themselves, in the ship, creeping about – boots off. Silently nodding to each other. The silent conversation over breakfast, when they first noticed Shirley was growing. That was the first conversation in months. Coming out of shock and fear. It broke the solidarity. And then they remember another conversation – from the planning of the silence.

'We thought if we broke the ship, we'd remember,' Drew says. 'That we'd get it back. Ourselves before the classroom.'

The ship settles again, suddenly, and the sound levels out.

'And we were wrong,' Alba says.

'And we were right,' Drew says. 'We remembered the white suit and Rufus and the Lotus and the Shop Around the Corner.'

'Are we going to die?' Alba says. She is sure she will lose her foot now. It has been scrunched at an odd angle for too long. To start off with she felt it go numb, then it pinned and needled but now, it just feels like it's gone. Like it isn't part of her anymore and maybe this is how it would be, little parts of her disassociating themselves with the whole of her. A foot and hand and then a forearm and a calf.

'I'm so hungry,' Stanley says.

'I'd eat almost anything at this stage,' Alba says.

'Remember cheeseburgers,' Drew says. And for a moment they are silent and think about cheeseburgers. They listen for them. Listen for them cooking and then for the noise they make as they're being put together. And then they hear them in their mouths the private noise when they chew. It has been a long time since any of them have chewed but also maybe they had breakfast that morning maybe this is all fast and happening quickly and they really have nothing to complain about because really a bit of discomfort isn't so much. Really. Like not so much.

'French fries,' Alba says. 'French fries.'

'How long does it take to starve to death?' Stanley asks.

'Days?' Alba suggests. Her hand is pressed against her cheek in an uncomfortable way and she's looking at it, wondering at its nutritional value. Now she thinks about it, now the conversation is live, it feels like there would be very little nutritional value in it, or in the act of eating something that was already 'you' but also, having to support one less limb – surely there is some biological mathematics in that? Surely if it didn't exist anymore and also you eat it surely there is some gain in that? Surely. Her hand is close to her face, she only has four fingers – her index finger on that hand has always been missing. Had always been missing since she got to the classroom. She lets her smallest finger slip into her mouth and rolls it around a bit. Her tongue seeks it out and plays with it and then she lets her finger play at her cheek and then she bites down hard on it. As hard as she can and it hurts and doesn't yield. There is no breaking it into anything useful. She sighs. She will try again, later. It's desperate now, but she has a sense, like perhaps all dying people do, that it is going to get more desperate and there will be need for it later. The finger, the hand. Possibly she can eat down to the elbow. But then what? What if she hits something vital and it bleeds out and then she dies anyway and the whole thing is for nothing? What then would be the gain? There will be no gain. But she leaves the finger in her mouth because it's warm and although she's thirsty it's wetter than the outside air and it forms some kind of closed system. Some kind of hopeful loop. Some kind of way back perhaps. A way back into the womb and she thinks about death again and what if it isn't the end. And she thinks about her mother who told her once and to her face about the abortion. That if she had been able to find someone to do it, she would have aborted Alba. Alba thinks about the space that holds up in her mind. The way she can't let it go. The way she's always thinking there will be some correction at some point. Some way of making her not exist anymore and this feels like it so it should come as no surprise at all. That it should come as no surprise that this is where she finds herself at forty-four years old – perhaps the only surprise is that it has taken this long to get here. Then she stops.

'I remember my mother,' Alba says.

'What?' Stanley says.

'I remember my mother.'

And they are all silent.

'Was she blonde?' Drew says.

'No,' Alba says. '*My* mother. I remember my mother. The one that is all mine.'

'My mother is blonde,' Drew says.

'My mother brought us baking sometimes,' Stanley says.

And they sit for a moment, remembering their mothers – not the ones in the Lotus or the apartments or sitting beside the bed where their son lay in a coma.

'Are we speeding up?' Stanley says. But it is really just to realign them, just to bring them all back into the fold, tuning up. Getting in line. Making sure they still resonate with each other – putting on the selves that resonate with each other. Doing this. For now.

If they could they would all look out the window and in their heads they do. These ghost bodies that have freedom of movement. These memories of bodies that fitted look out the window to gauge the speed even though there is nothing to gauge it against. Any memory of movement useless again. All reaching for it nothing but a habit of being freer. A lifetime habit. But really have they been that free?

'I think we're speeding up,' Alba says.

'What?' says Stanley.

'I think so,' Alba says. At first, it seems to be the best way to play as a team, realistically there is no way of knowing, probably they weren't speeding up. It doesn't fit with the physics or the machinery but she says yes to begin with. To agree with Stanley, but when he says, *What?* she realises, as if the words are magic, she really does feel the sense of speeding up despite what she thinks Stanley wants to hear. Most of it is in the sound. There is so much trickery in the artificial physics of the ship they will never feel it. Not until it's dangerous. Not until it's pretty much over. But the noise. It is building up in different ways now. Like more pressure is put on everything. As if it is calling out to the event horizon and the event horizon responds and in turn the noise in the spacecraft *Audition* is calling back – like they have been calling out for each other always, like they have finally found each other. Everything is frictionless but the way through makes more noise. It sounds like accelerating. But none of them have any way of reading anything to see if it really is. They have found themselves in corners far away from any controls or read-outs. Communication is lost.

They imagine they can hear the teachers every now and then, trying to call through, but even if it is real there's nothing they can do – shouting is pointless because there's no way of pushing the reply button. Alba is sure they are spying on them. Cameras, microphones. It makes sense except they all felt increasingly alone. Either no one was looking or the people on the ground were looking on in powerless shock.

They can imagine it.

All the normal-sized people in their white shirts and ties, because they too had a uniform. Headsets still on, or maybe headsets taken off and hung around their necks. Their horn-rimmed glasses – because surely they all have glasses, all of them staring in one direction. At a screen. A screen that shows all of the giants on the spacecraft *Audition* running, screaming. There is a lot of shouting on the screen. Some of the shouting is to try and help keep the spacecraft *Audition* operating, some of it is just shouting. Alba always panics in silence but even this tiny part of her seems lost now.

The sight of it. Not one of the ground crew will look at anyone else. They are too shocked. Can't take their eyes off. Because they know they are seeing something they will never see again. The acceleration of the growing, the panic, the screaming. No one gets to see this. So, they look and look. Maybe someone turns the sound down slightly because it's so worrying. Eighteen giants, getting more giant, running. Calling out in voices that change as they grow. Noises that no one has heard before. The sound of things being run over. The sound of doors being pulled out of their rails. The sound of some of them dying. Some of them? Most of them? And then, the control room on the spacecraft *Audition* is empty. And someone on Earth vision-shifts through the other cameras on the ship because surely, surely, they would never have let them go with no way of seeing what they were doing. The ship is worth too much. And they watch it now. The ship being ripped into pieces. Their crew.

And then, now being so at home with this scenario – it seems such a short step, not even a leap, a lean at most, to the fact this is an observation of what they thought would happen all along. This fast evolution they are building. This survival of the fittest. This extinction of any of them who can't make it. And maybe there is not so much shock or maybe the quality of the shock is different – that's what Alba thought when she first got stuck. Maybe the shock is that even with preparation it's still very hard to watch. That it's in fact worse in reality than they ever imagined, even though they've run it a thousand times in simulation. That maybe, even though they tell themselves they need to – maybe that it's imperative – it is nonetheless very hard to watch now it's unfolding in front of them. And Alba imagines they have seen far worse and imagines that none of the ships have got as far as *Audition*, that all the others are broken, the rest of the giants are dead. They are the last three left in space. By some random chance their trajectory was the one that lasted the longest and now it is over.

But then, Alba thinks, *No one is watching.*

The sound is even louder and nothing is working to bring on the numbness of the acceptance.

'It would be better,' Alba says, but it's useless. Something is broken, maybe they really are too far out of Earth's reach to make it work. It doesn't work at all. The sound just gets louder and louder. The ship hums. There is a heat to it but there is nothing to make this heat with. The heat is a quickening of everything. The quickness. But the sound has a heat to it as well.

They have no idea where the noise is coming from and now they really are getting uncomfortable. Now they really are feeling it in their bodies, maybe it is all made up of the noise. Maybe the noise is leading the physical sensations. But they are very much full of it. The speed. The hurtling. All of them are bracing now. Bracing for the inevitable breaking apart whether it comes from hitting something big or whether it comes from the final inability of the ship to stay together. It will surely pull apart.

None of them think to say goodbye to each other. When the end finally looks like it is here none of them wants to say anything. All they want is silenced by their own private, distinct regrets. As the ship gets louder and louder it feels like the silence of death will be such a relief they don't even dread it. Or maybe they can't actually believe this is the end. Maybe they are fooled. They have been fooled so much. So often something has looked like one thing and then it turned and had not been that at all. And maybe this is the next thing in that. Maybe the end is not the end. But still they brace themselves.

And as if seeing they are ready the ship shakes and there is a crash. A crash of sound. Like the air itself is trying to wrest the ship – so small in the vastness, so huge on Earth but so tiny now – from the sky, from its path. For millennia small humans have been fighting the huge weather. Strapping themselves to the masts of ships and they feel all that now. Like the terror is so great that it has stayed in them. Stayed in their bones and blood. This elemental fear. This strange weather – the weather of space.

'Is it a planet?' Alba shouts. The noise rings out around them, like the friction of metal on metal. Like the parts of the ship are trying to escape the shape of the ship. The brightest orange light comes at them from any opening in the ship, so they are all orange.

'What?' It is Stanley. He's heard – surely he's heard – but Alba can't fathom it. She's scared that if her attention goes anywhere except holding the ship up, together, whole, it will be over. It's like she's keeping them together with her mind. They all are.

'A planet!' Alba shouts. Her face presses hard against the wall, she is shouting it into the metal of the ship. She can feel the shout coming back at her. 'Are we going to crash into a planet?'

None of them knows anything. Alba is shouting for the company. All the others are silent to save themselves and Alba is loud. They have tried to make them all the same but when the ship starts to jolt they are all very different. Then it drops. Everything drops. Long enough for Stanley to say, 'I don't know,' and then some.

And then, like it hits something, but of course, it hits nothing, it jolts and shakes again. And then, maybe some centring thing is fallen off, they begin to spin, slowly at first but then very fast. The whoosh might have been in their ears. Their blood. There is hardly any space but they still slam against the ship with each rotation. The gravity is lost at certain points of the spin, there are moments where they are in free-fall and it feels like floating but for the tightest of time.

And still the shaking, still the grind of the pieces of the ship. Somewhere down the hall a bed comes free, or a desk, and is thumping now. Smashing apart, the sound changing as it breaks. Like the ship is sucking it down to its nub. And it rattles now, because it is so many small things. Shaken. And then another drop. And at the same time the whine of the engine, trying. Trying. But what? To right itself? They are the pilots and they are stuck and miles from anything that can help. They are powerless. None of them can surrender. Every ounce of them is trying to make sense of it. The sound is coming from everywhere. There is an almost stereo effect of the sound pulling from one ear and then the other. The movement and the change in pressure and position is blocking and unblocking their ears and all their balance is gone. No one knows what way up they are because the gravity is switching on and off – unable to keep up with the spin and the shake and the speed. They are all sure they are still going very fast. So fast. Alba vomits. Then Stanley hearing the noise vomits as well – and now there is the vomit and the piss and the sweat and the noise and the spin and the smashing of the soft bodies against the hard ship. And that has its own sound. A sort of ringing through their bodies. Drew is the only one who hasn't vomited now but it is taking all her energy. She was on a boat once. But this is not a boat. This is a remaking, a reshaping. It feels like birth.

Then there is another noise.

A hammering,

or a drumming

or a heart beating faster and faster

or maybe it is beating so fast

and so soft that it hums.

It is softer.

They can hear it, but it isn't over the other noise, it's under it, like it's wiping things away, calmly speaking to them, *In your mind you have capacities you know.* It is quiet and soothing and it moves through the loud and the frightening noises almost dampening them. It's like it is turning them all down as it moves toward and through them. Like it's visiting each of the sounds in turn and soothing them with some kind of friendly stroke. The whine of the speed is still there, they are still going very fast and spinning but all the edges are coming off it. And the grind of the metals – it's all still there but smaller, being pushed away as this new group of sounds arrives. Like they are growing out of the ground of all the other sounds. But this is wrong. It can't be compared with anything they have seen – it isn't a picture. It doesn't sound in a visual way. It is all in sound. It only exists in sound. The experience is like nothing they've felt before. Nothing. It takes up a new space. They can't feel it – they hear it though. It isn't a translation into any other sense. And it takes over everything. It isn't pushing aside the other sounds because it doesn't take up space. It is sound and it is soon everything. All of them have to face all of them. They are separate again. Like all the work of the classroom is wasted. Like everything from the classroom falls from them.

They realise it, it is dawning on them, but Alba whispers, 'We're free,' and it is real. Everything is so quiet but in a way that is full of noise. Alba is able to move her arm slightly and she can hear every part of the movement, not just the sound of her sleeve on the trunk of what remains of her jacket but the bones, the blood, the muscle. All of it. But it is almost silent – like everything that is silent takes the most attention. Like it pulls you closer, the quieter it is. Like it takes up more of your attention when it is quieter.

They are still going very fast – faster than they should be able to go. And now the ship is orange and there are flames as they hit the spin of the event horizon. Everything expands in the suddenly hot and now there are clouds and now they are plummeting. Still spinning, ground sky, ground sky, maybe a desert land, maybe some green. Maybe colours they've never seen before because the ground flashes past them – everything flashes past fast and then is gone. The ground is getting closer and it is like every colonial story but this time the land very much is going to kill them. It will eat them up and one day someone will stumble on the remains of the ship – huge – and then all three of them, squashed into their corners. With not even enough room to bleed. Dead with the shock of it. Ground sky, ground sky. Maybe trees, maybe a sea, they are so dizzy they can't tell what is seeing and what is memory, what is history, what is future, large creatures out of all proportion with the land and sky speed past them, through them. With no crash they carry on. And the whole time the strange new sound, quiet and heaving, holding them almost, percussive in turns and harmonic, almost squealing, but the most beautiful sound. That is what it is. Alba closes her eyes. It is a beautiful sound. There has been so much hardship and now there is beauty. And they are the ones that have made it there. And now as they get closer to the end, to the beginning, they start to call into the sound in reply. Humming, a small squeal of their own. A small outburst of air in the shape of a *huh*. A huff. The air from their lungs forced through their vocal cords. A vibration of a deep groan for in the end this is what it is. A deep, deep groan. Loud perhaps because of their size but all scale is gone now. All scale. Just sound, their bodies dissolve into it. Any sky, any land, any history, any future, falls away.

And then all the sounds fall into line. Harmony. And one clear voice calls out. It is an old song, or maybe a song from the future. *Calling occupants of interplanetary quite extraordinary craft*, the most beautiful voice calling out. And the spin slows. Everyone slows. *You close your eyes, you concentrate. Together, that's the way.* And then a guitar break. And then everything slows further. Or it feels like everything slows and the dark gives way to light. Beige and pink and all the pastel colours. The brightness fills the cabin. It soaks them as the song goes on and on and finally they start to hear exactly what it is telling them to do. And it hits them.

'We are the aliens.' Alba says so quietly but they are all thinking the same thing and hear her. It is like she is making audible what all of them are thinking.

We are your friends.

And they all try together. The song is an instruction, and they all try hard to transmit thought energy far beyond the norm, *We are your friends.* Everything is peach. Everything is smooth and soft, it invites them in.

The sounds are all over them, they feel comfortable for the first time. It warms all of them. All the pain is gone and they start to telepath messages through the vast unknown. Everything will be fine. For the first time in her life Alba feels like it will all be fine. Their craft is held and safe and they are held and safe in it. Alba starts to laugh. Uncontrollably. She watches Stanley rocking his head back and forth in time to the music. They realise there is room. The walls of the ship dissolve around them and they all cry now, crying with huge smiles on their face.

Alba holds her hand in front of her face, like she's never seen it before. They are floating now. There is peach and the palest of blue and some colours they have no words for. And the warmness that fills her is calming and bright and the happiness flows through her and the softness of the voice, the clarity and the melody of it. There isn't a note of dissonance in it. Alba tries to summon the moments before, tries to find in her body the remnants of any fear or pain but it is all gone. Like it lies on the other side of the gate. As she slowly rocks she tries to look to where they were but it is gone. There is nothing but the right-now. And the love. Alba sighs out. The ecstasy is held in place by the sweetness. There is no sign of any kind of tension or release, it is all release, it is humming through her.

Please come in peace we beseech you.

But anything else seems impossible. They're holding each other now, but even their bodies are dissolving, surrendering themselves away. And then it hits Alba, but in no means in a sad way, that before the classroom she hadn't been working in a small independent book store in New York, or with Rufus in an elevator, or on the side of the road as the Lotus Esprit bunny-hopped past. Before the classroom, they were in prison. Nothing metaphorical or allegorical – just a regular prison.

2

The event horizon is the ultimate prison wall
— one can get in but never get out.

Avi Loeb, chair of astronomy at Harvard University

before the classroom

The problem was everything was a drag. There was no respite in sleep. Alba knew she'd done something wrong. All of them did, they all knew probably they *were* wrong. Like, to the core. She'd hurt people. Sometimes on TV nice, middle-class people said this. 'I've hurt people.' But she had really hurt people. She'd beaten another women within an inch of death and that was only one thing, one of the things that got her into prison. She was lucky, that's what the judge had said. She was lucky.

'Not as lucky as her,' she'd said, and her friends had cheered and laughed from the viewing gallery.

But all the charge went out of her when he said, fourteen years. She was thirty. And as she was led away she looked back and all her friends were looking at their phones now. Onto the next thing. None of them would remember her. She didn't get any mail. 'Mail is for pussies,' she said, every time she didn't get any mail which was every time the mail came.

Sometimes it was her humour that got her through but not really. No one found her that funny. She lost a couple of teeth and then someone cut off her hair in her sleep, just to let her know. That something so sharp had been that close to her face and her neck. Slowly all the puff went out of her. Slowly, not quick enough for her to avoid a couple more beatings. But after a few years, eardrum blown the fuck out, index finger missing, knuckles broken and flat, she just got quiet. People who she knew on the outside came in now and didn't recognise her. Walked past her in the hallways. Connections were everything in prison but people saw no power in being friends with her. She got quiet. In the loudness of the prison she just got quiet. It was bliss for a while. No one even knew she was there and then, every now and then, someone did. Someone bigger than her. Realistically, by now, with any confidence beaten out of her, everyone was bigger than her. But this person was physically bigger. She called her out over the yard one day. Alba ignored it for a minute but the woman persisted. 'Alba!' she shouted. 'Alba, for fuck's sake.' So, she looked up and acted out that she had just heard her name. That she didn't realise. 'There's so much noise,' she said as she ran over. 'My ear,' she pointed at the ear drum that had been blown out and realised straight away how stupid she was because now they knew. But she could still hear them, even if they tried to sneak up on her. She knew.

When she got there the woman whacked her closed fist across the face. It hit her ear again. Alba rubbed it. The grey marl sweatshirt of her uniform was too big for her. Her hands never made it out of the sleeve and it was like this, hand still inside the cuff, that she rubbed the side of her face. That was all they'd wanted. 'You can go now.' Alba stood there, rubbing her face, one eye streaming, but that was all they wanted. Just to call her over. Probably if she'd come over straight away they would have been happy to just make a joke about her height, or her weight, or her hair, which never really grew back in any real way because it was a tradition now – cutting it off while she was asleep, while she was pinned down – but she'd made them look stupid by not responding immediately. It looked like defiance but really she'd just misjudged the whole thing, thought she could get away with it. That was one of the hardest things. Alba had no idea from one minute to the next what the right thing to do was here. It was completely unsettled. She'd been there a long time but had never got the hang of the place. What worked yesterday didn't work at all today. And every situation required an immediate response. If you waited a split second it might be seen as a decision and general affront but sometimes, the split second was exactly the right thing to do.

'Fuck off,' the woman said. And Alba jogged her heavy, short body back over to the other side of the yard where she'd been, by herself just sort of walking back and forward head down watching her feet – like a bear in a cage at a zoo.

'Alba.' It was a guard now. They were supposed to call you by your last name, but this guy was a sleaze.

'Hm,' Alba looked up this time, straight away and as she did, he smacked her across the face in almost exactly the same spot.

'Don't look at me.'

It was a different type of conversation. He was talking to her but she was not supposed to show that they were talking to each other. He wanted a blow job. He'd meet her in the toilets in five minutes. Alba didn't have a watch. He was a fuckwit. She thought about showing him her wrist. He left. She looked around the yard, no one had a watch and there were no clocks on the walls and all she wanted was to be alone. She let out a small groan and walked toward the toilets. Another guard asked where she was going and she pointed toward the toilet. And the first guard yelled from across the yard, 'I'll take her.' When they got past the door and no one could see them he hit her across the back of the head. 'I said five minutes,' he said. And she nodded.

The toilets had half doors. And at any minute someone could have walked in and probably no one would have given a fuck. His cock tasted musk. Someone had told Alba that musk came from deer so as her jaw ached and locked and he forced himself deeper and deeper into her throat, hand at the back of her head, she thought about a forest and a deer and a bear that was free now. She'd never seen a bear except Winnie-the-Pooh but she imagined there would be snow and a hunter and then her mouth filled with the warm thick and she coughed and he had her throat and said in her good ear, 'Swallow it.'

It was time to go in as soon as she got back to the yard. Alba had no friends. Other women had friends. They hung out. Called each other mum and sis but Alba had no one. No one could make her out, 'You Māori?' one of the skinheads had said to her and she'd shook her head. 'But you're not white,' another skinhead said. 'Hey whitey,' someone else yelled out at her and she shook her head. Her dad was Mexican. Her grandmother was a Gypsy. 'You can't say that,' Stanley said one night while they were folding washing.

'What?' Alba said.

'That word,' Stanley said. 'It's not a good word.'

'Oh,' said Alba.

'Romani,' Stanley said.

'Oh,' said Alba. Generally, other people explained her back to herself. Her mother told her she was fat. The teachers told her she was trouble.

Stanley had arrived on a Thursday. The women had spotted him as soon as he'd walked in the door. He was going to have more trouble than Alba ever did. Alba had seen that. She'd seen it before. There were two prisons and somewhere – on a birth certificate probably – it said Stanley belonged in this prison. But the birth certificate was wrong. It had assumed something that was blatantly untrue and even though Stanley knew exactly who he was they wouldn't change the paper and now he was here. The women called Stanley terrible things. Pushed him against walls and grabbed him. Probably Corrections had sent him here for his own safety. That's what they might say, but they knew he wasn't safe in prison – no one was. The other women were fascinated by him, but it probably wasn't even their fault. It was the ridiculous assumption made before he was an hour old, before he'd had a chance to introduce himself. Everything about the prisons was wrong so there were bound to be mistakes like this. Alba had seen it before. But now here she was making assumptions of her own. She knew nothing about how Stanley felt.

'How's it going?' Stanley had said a week or so after he got there. And Alba had looked around to see who he was talking to, she pointed at herself and Stanley nodded.

'Oh. I'm of no use,' Alba said.

'For what?' Stanley said.

Alba waved her arm around the dining room meaning, all of it – prison. 'I'm not connected,' Alba said. 'Or strong.'

'Fuck's sake,' Stanley said. 'It's not fucking *Narcos*.'

'Or like smart. Or a good conversationalist. Or um, nice, or friendly,' Alba started numbering it off, all the things she was not, then she stopped. 'I can fuck.'

'Oh,' Stanley said.

'Yeah,' said Alba, she knew there was something. 'I don't even make much noise.'

'Oh,' Stanley said, and he walked away from her and sat somewhere else.

Over the next few weeks they ended up in the same places together. There was a numeracy class. Some ladies came from outside to talk to them about maths. They tried to make it interesting, they had brought in a large, printed poster of a spiral. Didn't they want to get their Unit Standards? Didn't they want to be computer programmers when they got out? It was very boring and then Stanley asked to go to the toilet and a couple of minutes later Alba asked to go to the toilet and they snuck into the same stall and Alba said, 'Can I kiss you?' and Stanley said, 'Yes.' And they kissed for as long as they could – close, arms around each other. Ducked down slightly so they were out of sight if anyone should come into the toilet. The toilet was dirty but Alba was aware of none of it, just the cold porcelain that was somehow against her shoulder now, the chill shining through her grey marl sweatshirt. Stanley ran his hands through Alba's uneven hair, held the back of her head and pulled her closer into the kiss. Alba leapt slightly and Stanley pulled away. 'Sorry,' he said.

'We should get back,' Alba said, quietly, but they stayed ducked down – close.

There was so much noise outside the toilet they were in but Alba could hear everything Stanley said even in a whisper, and she leaned forward so their foreheads touched, the bridges of their noses, and they both closed their eyes and they could hear it all – someone crying, someone shouting, someone unhappy, someone powerful. But above it all they heard each other breathing and it was time to go back because their time was never their own, right now it was the maths ladies and then after that they'd need to go and eat lunch. No one trusted any of them with a second, but then when it got to a time when the guards wanted to go home, they would lock everyone in their rooms and what happened then was a free-for-all.

You were either locked in your room or you were a person locked in another person's room. You were either telling the people in the room what to do or you were the person being told. Alba had made a mistake when she arrived. Thinking she was the person telling people what to do but really, she never would be. So, in the room, when they were all locked down, her time wasn't hers there either. There was always something to do. And if there wasn't, there was talking. Noise. Sometimes, when Alba thought about killing herself, she wondered how much of it was just not getting any sleep. And then she'd think about how maybe death was just noise and being awake. She could fall asleep now. Here. Leaning into Stanley. Ducked down in the toilet stall. But they really should get back. Neither of them wanted to leave. Stanley smiled finally, pulling away and the cold rushed in.

'Come on,' he said, not happy about it but brave, so Alba would feel brave. 'Let's go.'

And it was like that for a while, smiles across the yard. No one wanted either of them so if they played it right they could be quiet and in a corner just talking. People still said horrible things to them. Alba still got hit. Someone held Stanley down and shaved off his beard with a disposable razor. But every now and then they could secret themselves away and just be together to talk and laugh a bit. It was the only time Alba smiled. She'd done it the first day in the stall and it had worried her, like something would break. But she did it quite a lot now. The sex was secondary but it was nice. The sex was a way of showing each other they were trustworthy. The undressing – although most of it was done clothed – the slide of it, the way they knew what each other smelt like. The way they knew what the other wanted, what made the other comfortable, safe, let their guard down. That sort of information was priceless in a place like the prison. Everyone was buttoned up – tight. Everyone was ready for action. And this is what they gave to each other: a moment of guard down. Fleeting minutes of not looking around. Or at least looking around with a smile on their faces. They would stand a long way from each other and talk. Alba would look at her feet. 'You have to stop doing that,' Stanley would say, if they had a private moment that wasn't only fucking. Alba would look at the ground. 'You'll give us away,' Stanley would say bending down a bit trying to get in

Alba's line of sight. Alba would look the other way.

Somehow, they both got a laundry shift. It was quite unbelievable because everyone wanted to work in the laundry and the likelihood of getting a shift with someone you liked was completely unheard of. But somehow it happened. 'Like we've pleased the Gods,' Stanley said and Alba laughed. They sorted clothes and moved them around the industrial-sized washing machines and dryers. They did well and they were fast within a couple of days. They didn't talk to anyone. People around them talked. They were as invisible as they could be. Every now and then something would happen. Someone not hearing them would be shouting as they walked round a corner about something that was private and then walk into one or both of them and then there was trouble because maybe Stanley and Alba had heard, definitely they had heard, but maybe they would think to tell someone. Information. And so the shouting person – who realistically if things were that private could have been talking more quietly, Alba said one day as she spat blood from her mouth – would punch them in the face. There was always violence. They were all in there pretty much for violence. There were people outside much worse for having met them. In the dark moments of the night they all felt the weight of this but in the bright day they wore it proudly. They had all been prey to it and they all perpetuated it.

Every now and then some princess would talk about victimless crime and all of them would want to kill her the most. 'There's no such thing as victimless crime,' someone big, someone high up would say. And if she knew what was best for her, she'd shut up.

Most people had forgotten about all of them. Most people. Visiting day was depressing. The prison was a long way from anywhere. There were no buses so even if people could get a

Sunday off work, or find childcare, first they needed to get enough money to get to the closest place and then there was nothing to do but walk. Alba's mother sometimes hired a car and she told Alba this when she got to the prison. Over and over again, and then when she left she would say something like, 'Well, that wasn't worth the car hire.' Alba was pretty sure she hadn't hired the car. Alba's mother had a way with words. She could convince anyone of anything and a daughter in a prison miles from the nearest train station or bus stop was a pretty good sell.

Alba had no idea what her mother was up to mostly and mostly when she came to visit it wasn't really to see Alba. There was always someone else in the visiting room who she was looking at and maybe even passing messages to. Often she would ask Alba to take a note to one of the other women. She'd give it to Alba under the table and Alba would nod. But as soon as she was out of sight, Alba would tear it up as small as she could and eat as much of it as possible. Then, of course, someone would come to her expecting the note and Alba would shrug. She had no idea what the repercussions were because she never read the notes but she imagined her mother would not be happy.

Alba's mother had wanted an abortion. Most of the mothers wanted an abortion but it was harder to get than you thought. Alba had wanted an abortion and was able to get one but not before telling a lot of lies to a doctor and then a psychologist. She'd had to tell them everything. All she wanted was to be rid of the baby inside her. She looked at her hands and wondered what would be of her if her mother had been able to convince someone. And then she thought about her mother and realised, really, probably, her mother hadn't tried that hard to get an abortion. Because if her mother had tried hard enough her mother would have been able to get an abortion. Alba watched her mother talk a man into paying for the damage she had done to his car once. Alba had heard her mother explain to a teacher that Alba had been at school when she hadn't. Alba had seen her mother take clothes from one store back to another and get store credit. If Alba's mother had wanted an abortion, Alba's mother would have been able to get an abortion.

Stanley's mother brought them baking sometimes and it was confiscated at the guard house. Stanley's mother visited quite a lot. That was mainly because Stanley's mum had the money to visit and a car and also because she spoke nicely to the guards so she was never kicked out of the visiting room. Alba would watch Stanley with his mother across the room. 'You should meet her,' Stanley said one day. And for the first time it occurred to Alba that maybe this wasn't just a prison thing, that maybe this was something else. She shrugged. 'Maybe,' she said.

The library was shut but a trolley would come round on Thursdays with books. Sometimes they were at work but also Stanley's mother would send books. The guards would check them and if they were good Stanley wouldn't see them, so Stanley told his mum to send dumb books, so his mother sent books by women and the guards weren't interested in those. The books the guards liked were: *The Secret*, *I'm Ok – You're Ok* and anything that was a self-help book. So Stanley's mother started sending one of those in the package as a sacrifice and then a whole bunch of books that the guards wouldn't like. Really, Stanley and Alba didn't care what Stanley's mum sent. They were reading them like they were a drug, just something to escape the prison with. They read all of them but their favourite was a children's book about evolution. The mammals were interesting but they loved the illustrations of the strange life that came from the sea. The Precambrian gardens where the animals that looked like plants waited and washed with the tide.

They were allowed to take the books to breakfast sometimes and mostly it was this book they took but not always. They would read them and not talk to anyone. They would read them in the yard, when they went out for their hour of sunshine. Often it wasn't sunny. Often the sun had moved so low it was cold and damp but they would sit on opposite sides of the yard without hats or scarfs. In the thin marl sweatshirts and pants. Sometimes just in a T-shirt because someone had stolen their sweatshirt. The sweatshirt would never look like a theft. Someone or some people would come over and stand over them and say, 'I need your sweatshirt,' and Stanley or Alba would take it off and hand it to them. Sometimes, they would try to keep their sweatshirts, maybe just a look like, 'seriously?', but usually it was just quicker and less dangerous to give the person the sweatshirt and carry on in a T-shirt. Stanley had arms full of tattoos – expensive, beautiful tattoos. Stanley was stunning. Sometimes Alba would see him and the sight of him would take her breath away – but she never let on. Because of the risk of a sweatshirt stand-over it was always important to wear a T-shirt. To begin with some of the women wanted to see Stanley's chest. They would throw him against a wall and rip his T-shirt over his head. Alba couldn't stand it. If she was there, she'd shout that a guard was coming or that there was something incredible happening somewhere else that she could see happening. Sometimes it worked and when they stopped and no guard came, or when they came over to look and there was nothing, Alba would say, 'Oh, sorry,' or 'There was this really weird bird.' And someone would smack her hard across the face or throw her against the wall and pull *her* sweatshirt over her head and punch her hard in the stomach. It wasn't like, in these moments, she could take any kind of high ground or martyr status. There were many times she had been the one throwing people against walls. Or at least the one behind the one throwing people against walls. Sometimes she thought about how they were all scared that someone would hit them so they hit someone and that made them all scared that someone would hit them. She couldn't work out for the life of her how to stop it, it seemed like some sort of perpetual motion machine or like the place was driving it. The guards fucked them and hit them and no one came to visit and they were told they were terrible and it was boring and they were kind of not responsible to anyone and all these things seemed to fuel the fear and Alba, for sure, did not know which came first – but she suspected it was the fear.

When your sweatshirt went missing you weren't always given another one – that was up to the guards. So, you had to get another one from someone else, so you stood over someone for one. No one ever stood over you for a T-shirt but occasionally they would go missing. They all looked the same. It was one of the worst places Alba had ever been which was saying something because she had slept outside a lot, and once spent the night in the boot of car while people outside the car talked loudly about setting it on fire, but she hated the prison so much. Stanley had never been anywhere like it, he had grown up in a loving house with parents who understood and supported him. But it was bad, no matter who you were. Some of the women said they liked it, but Alba doubted this. This sounded like whistling in the dark. It sounded like something you would say if someone asked you what you thought of the place and you wanted to look brave.

If anyone had asked Alba she would have said, *I hate it*. But no one ever asked, no one she could tell the truth to. Her lawyer asked sometimes but really, just as a reflex, he didn't really want to know. 'I don't want to know,' he'd say sometimes putting his hands up like he was surrendering to an armed police officer. 'Don't tell me.' But this was usually when she was trying to confess or on the verge of confessing something that she wasn't in trouble for yet. She had done a lot of bad things and she lost track and sometimes she would give information before he had asked for it and he didn't want to know. He knew she'd done what he was defending her for but somehow he drew the line at knowing about the things he wasn't defending her for, 'Yet,' he'd say. 'That I'm not defending you for yet.' And he'd curse and shake his head. Job satisfaction looked like it was zero for him. Sometimes even Alba felt sorry for him but then she remembered he had a nice house and probably heat and maybe someone to hold close at night, he was young. Some of the other women talked about him like that, called him pretty, but Alba couldn't see it. He was pretty much always scowling. He was pretty full of himself. Like Alba had been before they kicked it out of her. So, she mostly just felt angry at him, like he had something she deserved. Like there was a finite amount of what people deserved going around.

'I hope you don't get what you deserve,' Stanley laughed.

They were pulling heavy wet bed sheets out of an old washing machine whose spin cycle was broken.

'God help you,' and he laughed.

Alba was complaining about her lawyer and what she thought she deserved and it surprised and hurt her that Stanley laughed at her. They fought quite a lot but it was always muted and never really allowed to get off the ground. One of the most dangerous things you could do in a place like this was show that you cared about anything, and they cared deeply for each other, despite themselves. It was frustration that made them fight. They only saw each other when someone else decided to put them in a room together and when no one else decided to get in the road, so it was ridiculous to have any ongoing resentment.

But, now, Alba thought of the books and the way Stanley's parents visited and the way Stanley would have somewhere to go when he left, and he would leave – soon probably – and she wouldn't ever – probably – and how could he understand and Alba told him that, but like this: 'What the fuck would you know?' And Stanley got angry, like from zero to fuming. He dropped the wet sheets and they landed on the floor with a dull splash that got Alba wet.

Alba tried again. 'How could you understand?'

'Understand what?' he said.

'What it's like,' Alba said.

'What what's like?' Stanley asked.

'Well.' Alba didn't want to say it because it had nothing to do with the fight and it wasn't true but she really also wanted to say it because fuck Stanley and fuck Stanley getting anything over her and fuck Stanley for making her care and fuck this place and even after this she could have not said it, but she said it, 'Well, you get to be a man – even though you're not.'

'Sorry,' Stanley said, and it was very clear what Alba had broken.

'Well,' Alba looked out across the laundry in pain like she was looking for an escape, from the realisation of how wrong she was. She had been trusted and loved. She had been given the opportunity to love. She had been granted a permission to all of him and in this terrible place of constant vigilance and performance had been given space to show all of herself. In this intimate display they had exposed their most precious secret – how they could be hurt. And, now, at the first opportunity, Alba had taken this information and used it to shut the door. On any view of Stanley of course, but ultimately to any access she had granted to herself. They had been able to be themselves and now at the first sign of trouble Alba became of this place.

'I think,' Alba said, 'I was wrong, when I said that.'

It was an instinctive response. The weak apology. She knew almost as it was leaving her mouth that it made things even worse. Stanley looked at her. It felt like the world was opening up and closing down at the same time. She would lose him probably but more than that she'd had a chance to be kind and instead she'd hurt him. She had made all of it mean nothing.

'I'm sorry,' said Alba, taking another inevitable, useless run at it, like the song needed to be finished, the dishes put away, and maybe as a final parting gift to Stanley. In the hope that when he looked back on it he could see it was Alba who was wrong. That there was nothing wrong in him. That all she could muster after failing so completely with the trust they had given each other was an empty apology, spoken in the language of anger management and group therapy and relapse prevention. 'I was wrong and what I said was wrong and I recognise it was hurtful because it was false but also because it was hurtful. And I will endeavour to not cause pain again but really,' and she looked at her hands now, 'really, it is extremely likely that I will cause pain again because I am not without fault. I am fallible. But I will try harder.'

Then Alba stopped talking. In her life she had talked a lot of people into a lot of things, she had talked her way out of things. She had manipulated people into believing things that weren't true – about themselves, about her, about the world. So, now seemed like a good time for silence. Just to let it sit. So there was room for Stanley to think, room for Stanley to make up his own mind. Maybe Stanley would punch her in the face. The silence was almost impossible to endure. Stanley didn't speak to her for the whole shift. And then the next day he walked away from her in the yard. And the next day he wasn't at work. And the next day he was at work but still didn't talk to Alba. And so, this was how it ended. Like this. And she understood that Stanley was doing the only thing he could because some things were unforgivable and what Alba had done was one of them.

Alba sat in the yard watching everyone running about. There was no sun and she had nothing to read, so she just looked at everyone, like it was TV. Any time someone looked at her she let her eyes drop. Making eye contact was dangerous. She was bored a lot now, without Stanley. It was a gnawing boredom that was made acute with loneliness and the pain of what she'd said, not because she believed it but because she wanted Stanley to be the one that was hurting, not her. In the boredom that stupid thing she said came in and in and in. With nothing to do, nothing to read, all the regret just knocked and knocked and eventually she would open the door the tiniest possible amount, just to peek at the laundry and to get one last look at the last moments when she and Stanley were she and Stanley. First, she'd play over the pile of laundry and Stanley, hold the memory still, maybe touch him, maybe remember what it was to be touched by him. But she couldn't hold it at bay forever and then it would play out. What she'd said, the sense it was wrong, the sense a moment too late that it was wrong. And it would hurt, like physically, and then the sting would go out of it. And when it did, because eventually it had to, other things came falling in. She thought about her crime – the one she was in for. The way Drew had cried and begged for Alba not to kill her and then all the other crimes, the way she stole her own grandmother's prescription pills, the way she stole from her mother's handbag, the way she hit kids at her school, the way she enlisted a bigger kid to hit another kid she thought she couldn't beat up. It all came falling in. And there was nothing she could do. This was maybe what prison was for, so she had to sit with it. So she had nowhere to go with any of it. So she was stuck here. And boy was she stuck. It was the worst kind of boredom, boring and dangerous. She needed to keep her guard up so she could stay safe and she was disinterested in everything, even in staying safe. It was a terrible few months. It would have been better if she had never met Stanley.

She pulled at her sweatshirt sleeve, it was cold and the wind was coming in on her wrists. If someone gave her the option, like, right now – to never have met Stanley, to forget everything – she would have said, *Where do I sign?* She pulled down on her sweatpants cuffs then again at the wrist and waistband of her sweatshirt. Her uniform didn't fit very well anymore. Someone had probably put it in the dryer for too long. But they were supposed to go in the dryer. Alba had lost her job at the laundry after she threatened to cut someone's eye out. They'd searched her cell, which no one in her cell was happy about. She had a bruise over her jaw and one of her back teeth had fallen out. Her sweatshirt didn't meet the waistband of her pants. She looked over at where Stanley was standing and he was doing it as well. The pulling, the tugging on the sweatshirt. Stanley had kept his job in the laundry. Alba was going to an anger management course. She wasn't allowed to do the maths anymore. She watched Stanley as much as she could now they didn't work together and Alba was at the other course, watching out for Stanley but also watching him. Missing him. Wondering what it was she needed to do, then realising there was nothing. If this was a romantic comedy there would be a reconciliation – a grand gesture, a revelation, running through an airport – and sometimes Alba entertained this, as a way to get her through a particularly tough afternoon but it was so much worse on the come down. On the realising there would be no reconciliation and that really it was all over. She would walk past Stanley sometimes while she was fantasising their beautiful reunion and she was sure Stanley could smell the hope on her but Stanley didn't even look up because probably Stanley had moved on. And then it would hit her, so much harder than if she hadn't hoped. So much harder. But she could never catch it on the way up.

Stanley left the yard. Just like that. As simple and as profound as that. He walked away. Passed Alba like it was nothing. Like it had never begun. Alba watched him walk away. She could do that now because Stanley really didn't see her anymore. It was that complete. So, Alba watched, like she was a ghost and as she was watching a guard came to her in the hallway, they were all in the hallway going to the places they needed to go and the guard said she was needed. Her lawyer. She needed to go with the guard. She didn't even worry about that. She didn't even need to worry about that. Because she almost hoped she was raped again. Raped to death. She missed Stanley and it was over and she needed to come to terms with it. She needed to do that – get back to that place. 'Come on,' the guard said. She was still watching Stanley or the space where Stanley had been before he went through the door, looking for something. But Stanley was gone and with him every trace of him. Gone. The guard grabbed her shoulder, then let it go in a shock, as if she were a hot stove and he looked at her. 'Are you taller?' he said. It was an accusation and she laughed at him. She didn't mean to or maybe a part of her meant to, she wanted to be hit that badly. 'Right,' she said. 'I'm forty,' she said under her breath as she walked past him to stand by the door he was leading her to. And he hit her across the top of her head. Whack. And the pain rang through her and it wasn't enough – it didn't come anywhere close to watching Stanley walk past her, not even noticing her. So, she walked some more, through the door. Down another hallway. Someone shouted at her from inside a cell. They would kill her and it was fair enough. Everyone should just kill her. It had been fine before Stanley, it had been sad but it had been fine. But now she'd had a glimpse of what it was like not be alone it was like the aloneness was terrible. Then she hit her head. It wasn't the guard. She'd gone to walk under the stairwell she'd walked under a million times and it hit her in the face.

'Come on,' the guard said. She was making him uncomfortable with her death drive. It was seeping out of her and if she died he'd have more forms to fill in. He just needed to get her to the visiting room so the lawyer could just talk to her because then it was someone else's problem and he could just go for a break. His wife had made him a sandwich, it would be terrible but it would be something. There were slushie machines in the staffroom but they were all turned off during winter and he didn't even want one. He did but no one needed to know how much he wanted one. But Alba knew. She could tell the story.

Alba's lawyer looked at her in an odd way. A similar way to how the guard had looked at her – there was a spark of fear somewhere. She knew she was frightening, was she more or less frightening without hope? Surely someone had done a study about it. Surely. The fear passed over the lawyer, maybe he had a sandwich somewhere as well, and he opened a folder.

Alba waited but no one told her to sit down. The lawyer was sitting down and when he looked up she was towering over him. 'Sit down,' he said. And she did, shifting a bit in the chair to get comfortable.

'There's a hearing,' he said. 'You're coming to the end of your non-parole period.'

Alba nodded.

'The victim wants to meet you. They want to deliver a victim impact statement.'

Alba shrugged. Nothing mattered.

'And that will be soon. And if I were you. Like my advice is that it would be better if you were quiet and listened and don't be threatening, because you don't normally get a chance to be in front of the judge again. Especially not this far into your sentence. Usually they forget about you.'

Alba didn't do anything, and he said, 'Do you understand.'

Alba didn't really understand but she nodded. Was he saying this was a chance to get out, or was he saying this was a chance to make amends with no real change to her life except maybe at a deep soul level which she really didn't believe in so it was really no big deal? But she nodded. Who cared? Like really, who? Alba didn't care, her mother, Stanley definitely not, and then who was there? The last person who cut off her hair? The guard that face-raped her? No one. The lawyer? There was plenty more work for the lawyer. So, she would just do what he said.

'I think you should do it,' he said. And she nodded.

'It'll probably be in the next few days.'

'I have a course,' she said and he looked at her in that way they often did, all of them – social workers, guidance counsellors, the women who came in as volunteers to show them how to make quilts – like she didn't understand. Like at some fundamental level she had misunderstood and was an alien to them. She was completely an alien to them. Like, go home, alien. Do you not get it?

'We can get you out of the course,' he said, almost mocking. Had he forgotten to tell her? The next few days seemed soon. Was the mocking to cover up that he'd forgotten to tell her? Was he mocking or was she just paranoid? Some of the professionals said she was paranoid, but she didn't think so. She tried to cross her legs under the table but the table was too short.

He thought he understood better than her. He thought that she thought she was getting something over him – or trying to. Like really trying to play him for a fool. To him, they all looked like one thing – none of them really wanted to do reconciliation. He thought, probably, if he was in the same situation, which he never would be, he probably wouldn't want to be face-to-face with the person who – Alba watched him check her notes – he'd hit multiple times in the head with a heavy object until it had broken and he'd resorted first to the splinters of the vase and then his bare, bleeding hands. Then he looked at her, involuntarily. He was looking at her before he could stop himself and he prayed it didn't show on his face – but Alba saw it. He didn't care what she did, not deep down, not in any serious way, but if she didn't go to the victim impact statement, he'd be fucked. If she didn't show up or if she showed up and was terrible, threatening, the judge would have something to say about it and then where would he be? He'd be fine but the next few weeks would be hard at work and it was hard enough at work. He thought he understood better than her, she could see it in him. But despite all this he didn't.

She was looking at him when he finally caught himself. If she didn't go to the course she would get kicked out of the course and the course paid and without the pay she couldn't buy tampons and then she would have a bleeding problem in a few weeks and she would have to stuff toilet paper into her vagina and she didn't always get all of it out and she didn't want to die of some infection from toilet paper.

But he looked at her like he was saying in his mind, *What the fuck?* I have friends who are property lawyers. A guy I was at law school with has five houses, and a plane. She thought she should tell him she could see it all, on his face, in the way he moved but then she realised she shouldn't because then what? He was on her side. It said so, in the pamphlet she got from the justice department, but he would also throw her under the bus given half the chance. It had happened to a friend of hers. Her lawyer had shown up hungover and angry. He'd asked her for a blow job and she'd said no, so he slammed her face-down over the desk and fucked her. There seemed to be no end to the men they were left alone with who would rape them.

They wouldn't let her be alone with Stanley. She'd thought about it and if she could just have a few minutes with him, just some time with no one else, just a few moments, like five minutes, she would be able to explain. That had been her problem on the day. She played it over and over, it was often all she did in a day. She spent whole weeks in that one five-minute block of their lives, and her biggest mistake was stopping talking. If she'd just kept going, not given any space, it might have all been all right. She ran her hands through her hair and the sensation exploded into her face – she hadn't slept in months. She could feel Stanley so close. She could feel him. Like she expected him to walk around a corner. Save her. But he was never going to do that. Ever. He was in the other room being called by his old, wrong name. Being told where to go. It was terrible. But there was nothing left for her to do because she had betrayed him. More than anyone else, possibly. She could feel the sadness rising in her cheeks. The erotic so quickly transitioned into shame. The possibility of the touch making starkly clear the absence of it.

She looked behind her lawyer. He was still talking. It didn't matter. She could pick it up later. She was trying to escape, really, couldn't be here, couldn't escape. Nothing. Trying to find the nothing inside herself, that small place that really wasn't there anymore but she still kept looking for. That private place that had been colonised by this place. No one was allowed anything for themselves.

It was hope that was the problem. That was why she'd been ostracised and beaten and left. Because no one could stand to see her hopeful or her stupid-faced. No one wanted that in their lives. And they thought she was lying. That was the hard part of it. Even Stanley. Stanley always thought she was lying. He would look at her like she was stupid and maybe she was. Maybe. It seemed logical and also, as the lawyer kept talking, fine. She had no problem with it. She searched inside herself saying over and over again, *I am stupid*, to see if there was any pain in it, but there was nothing. Not here, or here. So, she just put it on, like the rest of the information she was learning about herself. All from the outside as if she knew nothing. As if the whole world and everyone in it was her user guide. What would she know?

The lawyer had stopped talking now. He was looking at her so she nodded. 'You better not,' he said and it sounded like a precursor to more rape. Well, new rape, he'd never laid a hand on her but there was always a first time. That was how it worked, they drew you in.

'I won't,' she said.

And he said, 'Well stop nodding then.'

And she did.

He said they would come and get her and she didn't know what day he was talking about but it didn't matter. All the other women had noticed Stanley, all of them, because he was a man. It had been terrible for Stanley but then he'd found her, sought her out perhaps, recognised in her a type of invisibility that he needed or that he wanted. Saw in her a way to be seen correctly while not being seen wrongly. The women wouldn't leave him alone. They stayed away from him to start with. Sized him up – threat or pet. Some of them said he changed everything but that was ridiculous. Alba stayed out of it. All. Until that day, during the boring maths class, in the toilet. His hands clasping her face. Everyone had lost interest as soon as he was even hardly associated with her and that was how they had been able to carry on the way they did. But now, almost as soon as he left her, never to talk to her again, he became of interest again. He had positioned himself. She was pretty sure of that. Maybe it was because he needed to find a new way to organise his defences now they were finished but whatever it was, he had a lot of safety now. He was in with the right people. People who could protect him. It looked like it had cost him a lot. They were all walking past the room Alba was in now. The room was all glass, she watched out for Stanley for a glance of him smiling maybe, looking safe, not at ease, but not in danger. And it was the only thing that settled her. Watching him, safe. Thinking about the last time she saw him looking safe. It was what Alba had done that bound her to him. The way she'd hurt him. It was the same with Drew. It was an old and sick feeling. But her body was still made that way, with a looking out, a sense of ownership that made it hard to live with herself. Tied up in the change, the harm she had wreaked on people's lives and bodies now mixed with the disastrous love she still felt for Stanley. Every part of her body confused her, every thought.

Alba was as isolated as she always had been. She wasn't sleeping at all. First because she missed him but now because the tiredness was making her paranoid. Scared of what might happen if she did shut her eyes.

The next day, while they were in the yard, a guard called her last name from the gate. She looked up and he waved her over. She had court, what the hell was she doing here? So, it was true. She walked with the guard and was handcuffed and then the van took her to court. Her lawyer was there to meet her and was angry when he saw she hadn't brought a change of clothes.

'You look like a criminal,' he said.

'Yeah,' she said. Not being a smart-arse just confused, but of course he took it the wrong way and got angry. But then they were called in.

He didn't explain anything, so that must have been what he'd been doing when they'd talked the previous day. There was no point pretending so she just followed and sat when she was told to sit and stood when she was told to stand and then her victim came in and was identified. Drew stood in the dock and read from a piece of A4 paper which had typing on it. It had been printed out. Alba thought about how Drew must have typed it out on a computer and then printed it out and brought it here. Next to Drew was a plastic folder and she realised she must have put it in there to keep it from being crumpled. Alba could see the scar on the top of her head, the one that went into her hairline, and she remembered how it had felt, when that part of Drew's face had split open. They had been friends. The skin had popped. There was bruising and then there was blood. The blood had flowed. Alba looked at her own hands and she had trouble recognising them. She tried to look at Drew's face again but Drew looked up, so Alba looked down, they did it several times – an odd little dance. Alba hadn't heard her talk in years. The memory she had was of Drew shouting and begging. It was a strange experience. She knew it was Drew because she could see the scars she'd made but the voice meant nothing to her. Nothing. She tried to listen, she did a good impression of someone listening, but she couldn't take her eyes off Drew. The change Alba had wrought on her. The permanent damage which was to say the way she had created something new from her. It made a part of her rise up. Some creative urge that had been put there by the many beatings she'd received throughout her life. Like she had been taught by the violence. But she didn't let it show. There was a tradition, a ritual to court. She had been coming since she was small, she knew what was required of her and she could perform it easily. She kept her head bowed but also she looked up from under her fringe to watch Drew, the way her lips tried to get around her new teeth, the way it was hard for her to read. The way Alba had made that transformation possible. Alba felt like Dr Frankenstein to this new Drew. But no one would see her fascination because Alba's body language was practiced. She wouldn't need to talk. She knew that. They told her it would re-traumatise Drew, that all she needed to do was look like she was listening. But she couldn't listen, not for real. There was some truth to what they thought they were doing here. Alba couldn't live with herself so she didn't listen. She just watched. And in a way this had the effect they wanted because as she watched she saw what she had done, it played out in front of her and she felt it – deep inside herself. It was being imprinted on her as much as it was imprinted on Drew, it had changed them both. They were related intimately in this way.

Drew went on.

A lot of what she was reading felt like maybe it had come from a book Drew had read or a film she'd seen. It felt like platitudes. No doubt, Alba had ruined Drew in a very specific way but it was like she didn't have the words for this particular type of pain, there was a jargon to it all, because Drew also had a part to play. And Drew knew that. Alba imagined someone helping her with the statement. Someone sitting with her helping her come out with it, maybe showing her a selection of other statements that she might gain inspiration from.

And then finally, it was over.

Drew had cried and was wiping her face with the back of her hand. She was a retail worker, she was just walking home. They need never have met. There was no reason that they would have ever met that night. But then Drew had walked round the corner at the wrong time. Alba stopped. No, that wasn't it. It had the ring of truth, none of it could have been denied. But they had known each other for years. Alba had waited for her. Drew had mouthed off. That was the problem. Like obviously if she hadn't been there then Alba wouldn't have attacked her. But if she hadn't been there, Alba would have found her somewhere else. Alba had been sent to do it because Drew was her friend and Alba had vouched for her. But Drew could have easily been there and got home safely if she hadn't opened her mouth and if it hadn't got back to the people who Alba vouched for her to. And if the world was different.

When she'd found Drew, that night, she'd tried to reason with her, but Drew was drunk and arrogant. She'd called Alba white trash. It wasn't the trash that worried Alba. She knew what she was, she didn't have any delusions of grandeur. Alba was light now, now that her mother had bleached any ounce of her father out of her, but she wasn't white, it wasn't that simple. And to have Drew call her that, when she'd come to try and work something out, was just too much. It shouldn't have been. It would have been great if she could have held herself. When she did anger management they talked about things floating off her like water off a duck's back, but it didn't feel like that would ever be possible for Alba. Like there was a reason water flowed off a duck's back and she just didn't have that going on. She was not Teflon. Everything stuck. She could remember things people said to her when she was five years old. She'd never done anger management before she came to prison.

She pulled her sweatshirt down. Everything was riding up and her hair was getting short. Parts of it used to touch her shoulders. Maybe it was a new game. She could see out of the corner of her eye that the judge was watching and she realised she'd let her remorse drop. It was hard to have remorse when really you hadn't done anything wrong. She agreed she could have handled the situation with more subtlety, with a better attitude, but Drew had really been asking for it. Alba had vouched for her and they'd done the job and then Drew had blabbed and it had got back to the people Alba worked for, and anyway it was done now. The whole exercise seemed ridiculous really. Like what difference would it make? Then she remembered that everyone needs their pound of flesh. The waistband on her sweatpants was digging in and at the same time they were hanging well below her waist. Nothing fitted any more. Nothing. The sweatpants rode up at the bottom and down at the top. It didn't even make any physics sense.

It wasn't over. Drew had started talking again, she was reading and crying now and Alba nodded making her face as sad and remorseful as she could. Like what Drew was saying was making her hate herself but it was a waste of time because she really thought more and more that she had done nothing wrong. Drew hadn't learnt a thing, she was still condescending and rude and now she thought she had a reason, it was pointless but Alba had to hold all that at bay. This and missing Stanley. It all needed to be held at bay. If she could just hold it together for however long it took Drew to read the paper. She looked up slightly, in a kind way, to see how many sheets Drew had left but she had been putting the sheets to the back so it was impossible to see how many more she had to go. Maybe she wouldn't stop when she came to the first page. Maybe they were in a loop and it would be never-ending.

Drew pulled at her shirt. She was wearing a white shirt, like she was a businessman. She wasn't a businessman. The bottom of her shirt was coming out of the top of her pants. She kept trying to tuck it back in but it kept coming out as she moved. It was short. She'd bought it too short. Alba's feet hurt. Her shoes didn't fit properly. Drew pulled the cuff of her shirt down, back down over her wrist. She didn't stop reading. She held the papers in one hand and pulled down the cuff of that sleeve. She had bought the shirt too small. Alba had to stop herself from laughing because she saw what it said about Drew, the delusion she had about herself. The fact she thought she was so small but she was big. She was getting bigger.

Alba looked again, all the game of looking remorseful fell out of her as she did.

Drew was getting bigger.

When she'd started the statement Alba couldn't see Drew's belt, but now it was a few inches above the dock. Alba looked around the court but no one else had noticed. Drew and Alba were the same in this way. Alba looked at the dock in front of her. Her hands had been joined, holding each other, since she got there, it was part of her remorse act. They had gently rested on the dock when she'd arrived. Now she tried to let them rest again. She leaned forward but it was too far. She couldn't get them to rest in the same way. She looked around. No one was looking, not even the judge now.

Even the judge thought Drew's statement was going on a bit long. Alba could see that. He was slightly nodding off. Not actively, just, his mind was wandering. Maybe to lunch. Alba looked at her shoes, the stitching was puckering slightly under the pressure of her smallest toe. It looked like they couldn't hold. This was a problem. Corrections didn't cover shoes, she would have to try and get her mother to send new ones but she would probably need a new size. Drew pulled at her shirt again. They shared that discomfort. She had rearranged Drew's face and now they were both growing. Was it a punishment? Drew didn't deserve punishing – Alba could see that– she wasn't a monster. But then, was it a gift? Alba's life was te rrible but she was pretty sure she hadn't done anything to deserve a reward. It made no sense. But then Drew pulled the cuff again and there was the tiniest sound and the sleeve had come away from the yolk and Drew looked up to see if anyone had noticed and looked Alba straight in the eye and they both knew at that moment that their perspective was changed. Each of them knew the space the other took up and that had changed. No one else would notice. This was the relationship of victim and perpetrator. They knew each other better than almost anyone. It would be a few weeks before anyone else noticed, they could see that too. It was relatively easy to gauge when it would become noticeable to other people. Both of them had become intent studies of other people because of that night and they were linked in that way too.

Drew stopped talking.

It took a minute for the judge to notice. He was paying that much attention to something other than Drew, and he said, 'Miss Blanchfield?'

'I'm done,' Drew said, because she had a scheme beginning. She knew how strong Alba was, she'd felt it herself and Alba could see it all spinning in her brain. Maybe they would stop growing tomorrow but maybe, maybe they wouldn't, and that was what excited Drew. She looked over at Alba so that Alba knew she would see her again. Alba couldn't smile because it would break her veneer of remorse but she made a slight lift in her eyes so that Drew could see. They would take over the world. It was very clear now. They would have all the power. The judge would listen once she was gigantic. They could both see that. Once they were large, no one would dare look away.

'Thank you,' the judge said.

Alba wouldn't get a chance to speak and if she did it was important that she didn't say anything. It was all up to the judge but it was getting on to lunch time and he had a lot of work to do so he just said everyone could go.

The prison guard who had come with them led Alba away and her lawyer went to find his next client.

in the first room

Stanley and Drew look at Alba and she feels a rise in her neck and cheeks.

The space the three of them are in is soft in its pinks and purples. It is thick in its air. The falling stopped, the images of the prison and the crime and the court gone, they seem to have come to a stillness. It feels, to Alba, like a conversation – the spinning, the falling, the way the story was whispered into them. The story that came to her as they fell feels like truth that asks, *What now?* The way she is sure they are all reorganising what they think is real about themselves feels like a conversation with some unknown fourth party – like it's being offered. Alba feels the way they are apart now. The other two wary of her.

Maybe because he truly is questioning it but probably because he wants to hear Alba admit what she's done, Stanley says, 'I feel nothing for you.'

'Likewise,' Alba lies. She doesn't want to show her hand yet. What they saw as they fell is true. And it would be stupid for a person in her position – revealed, exposed as a terrible person – to give anything away. And maybe this is something of her true self coming out, resurfacing. The criminal mind. She feels the scheming rising in her. And then she sees it, a last offering from the unknown part of this conversation. She sees it, the final extent of her height. The biggest she got on Earth.

'We were big,' she says. 'There were several guards and they all had pepper spray and like some kind of superheroes me and Stanley were swatting them away like a normal-sized person would swat away flies and we were breaking our way out of the prison. Breaking walls, kicking at anyone who came in our road and we were running through the green hills that surrounded the prison. Into the grey sky that came down lower and lower toward us, we were laughing and holding hands.'

'And then the helicopters came,' says Stanley, 'and the gunshots. Only aimed to floor us. The first few not even registering and then finally as more and more people came I fell first and you came back to hold me and then more and more, and you fell too – beside me. From the prison, as other folk sprawled out of the openings we'd opened, we must have looked like some mythic new shape on the hill. A new peak or range.'

A tear slips down Stanley's cheek and Alba reaches out to touch it and Stanley pulls away and the true nature of their time before the classroom keeps coming.

Drew had visited every weekend. First just Alba, but as Stanley grew, eventually Drew organised for Stanley to join them. They would all try to slouch, to look shorter as they grew. On the outside, Drew was able to make new clothes. First letting seams out and then buying fabric, walking carefully down the narrow aisles of the sewing shops and then ordering online from the only part in her room she could fit in now. At first the sweatshirts and pants had stretched to accommodate Alba and Stanley, going from baggy to tight to midriff and then they didn't cover anything. Stanley did it first, Alba saw him from across the yard. Two sweatshirts, then three tied together by sleeves to cover as much as he could. Alba copied him, although it was harder for her to get the extra sweatshirts.

When she visited, Drew would talk to both of them but Stanley still wouldn't look at Alba, wouldn't speak to her, spoke like she wasn't there and he was talking just to Drew. Sometimes they would talk about Alba like she wasn't there. When Drew left, everything went back to how it had been, how it was – Stanley acting like Alba didn't exist. But on Sundays the three of them would sit in the corners of the visiting room. Sit on the low chairs to try and look smaller than they were but they were scheming. It became clear that they were going to take over the world.

The guards had noticed a few weeks before they broke out. Drew came to the visitor's check-in, and the guard said, *No.* They already had a plan though. They planned it by the moons. In code. Alba was the polar bear, Stanley was a grizzly. Drew wrote them letters signing her name like she was a wolf. She was squirreling away money, she'd bought a car, she'd found them a place to hole-up. The moon was the constant they relied on. On the night of the day Drew didn't come to visit they would look up and wait for the full moon then three nights after the full moon, when the evening sky was at its darkest, they would run in the direction of the highest hill they could see and Drew would meet them there.

They were too big, that was why the guards had stopped Drew's visits. They were behaving as well as they could but everyone was scared of them so everything they did looked like a threat. They were breaking things just in their everyday activities. Once they got to the classroom – which was of course another prison – they realised there were hundreds of them, that a plan had been in place but no one had told the guards or the head of the prison. Alba imagined the head of the prison calling and calling but no one would take his calls and no one wanted to help. But there was a plan in place. It became very clear when they got to the classroom – separately – because by the time they got to the classroom the forgetting was already complete. On the first day they were sat together, the three of them, and instead of, *Let's run*, they said, *Nice to meet you*.

All of them had pretty much given up by the time they got to the classroom. That was the smart thing about it all. Early on, after watching them for a while – all of them – growing, one of the people who weren't growing would have noticed the type of people they were. How all the people growing were people who were used to being told what to do. Who didn't hold out much hope. They had fought and had to be restrained but after orientation – after being talked to for days on end, into the nights – they started to see things differently, like, literally. All the scheming talked out of them. Any memory of how powerful they thought they were going to be together gone.

Now Alba remembers it.

It was a seamless balancing act between not wanting to be hurt anymore and being told nothing was hurting them. No one asked questions. But also, after a while there didn't seem to be a right question to ask. What was a question anyway? Everything felt off but that was the nature of things.

Life is suffering, one of the special speakers had told them, headset microphone on, wandering the huge stage, hour fourteen of a seminar where they were only allowed to go to the toilet when someone said they could and they only ate what was given to them when it was given to them. The exhaustion was real but the speakers never got tired. They were always fresh and maybe they were different people but also maybe they were all the same person. It was all a blur. And life was suffering. And here they were suffering so maybe that was life, and then there had been Torren and the breaking in and getting ice cream and the lying in the dark outside under the large sky and no thought of escape, like it had all been worn out of them.

'It's genius really,' Drew says. 'When you think about it.'

They all nod.

'We were too big to control physically. There was no room to kill us.' The light is soothing and they can feel it in all their limbs, it makes small plush noises in their ears. 'Physical room,' Drew says, to clarify. 'Not ideological or political or cultural. There was no physical space. We were huge. You saw us all,' she points to her head, to show she means in the memories that had come back to them all as they fell. They see how huge they are in the memories. Like the memories are currency. Every word is important, every clarification makes them whole again. Telling them back to themselves. 'We were gigantic.'

The space they are in has nothing to gauge any height with. Alba is looking around, hoping, probably all of them are hoping. But there is no way to tell. All they want to be is small again and maybe the whole thing has shrunk them back.

'Are we dead?' Alba says. She's looking around, the idea of who she was is coming back to her. She finds her way back into her body the way she used to be in it. At least, she hopes that is what it looks like. To Stanley. That she is coming back into herself. Little wonder he hadn't recognised her before, now he can see her, looking around, asking if they are dead. Hoping seeing her like she was will cause him to perhaps feel a rise in himself. Erotically, not angrily. But that seems like more than she deserves. Stanley isn't even looking at her.

'Hello?' Stanley says. But of course no one replies. They're alone. At least it feels that way to Alba.

'Do you think they speak English?' Alba says. Stanley shrugs. There was the song, but did they even know what that meant? Maybe the hosts don't even exist. Maybe they've already left. Maybe it's some kind of ancient trap, remaining long after the setter is gone.

'Why do you think it's a trap?' Drew asks.

It appears nothing is private anymore.

'Well,' Alba says, because this is the way of things now. 'They sent the song?'

That seems right. But where are they?

'Maybe we're going to die,' Alba says. Which seems like a big probability. They are alone in the huge room. The word 'room' seems so wrong. There are no walls or end to it. They are standing. Like, the sensation is standing but there is no floor. There is nothing but the light as it plays on their skin and in their ears and there is nothing else. The light slowly rotates through several pastel colours. It is almost a full pastel spectrum.

'Maybe this is them trying to talk to us?' Stanley says, lifting his hand in front of his face to watch the light play on it. They all try very hard to concentrate toward the light but there is nothing. Nothing they can sense. It is very clear that what they can sense is not a good judge of any space they're in.

They'd wrecked the ship. They would never be home again but, really, Alba had known that the whole time, they all had. And maybe now they're dead in some alien heaven.

'For fuck's sake, Alba,' Stanley says. Stanley's book smart. That's what Alba thinks as she looks at him. Maybe he's practical as well. Those two things weren't mutually exclusive but she knows he's book smart because she's seen it. In action. And it seems that book smart – philosophical thinking – is what the moment needs. Alba notices how comfortable she is. She feels like she's in the afterglow of good sex. They're standing up but there's something to the atmosphere that's holding them up, cushioning. Alba wonders how it would feel to move about. She jumps and it feels great. She jumps again and then she turns around on the spot she's in and then she takes a very large step.

The others are standing still. Drew's arms are folded over her chest like she's thinking. Stanley has his hands behind his back. Alba keeps jumping and she gets higher. She's sure of it. She thinks about being very high and she gets very high. But the others aren't paying any attention. She's suddenly hungry and thinks about eating and is full. The others are still thinking about what to do next. She thinks about her insides and needs to wee and then she feels the comfort and satisfaction of having urinated. It seems that there is only aftermath here. It beats the prison. She can see that now and she shuts her eyes tight and imagines that final run up the hill into the green, it was dark, the clouds were low and the view as they looked back just before the shooting started was magnificent even in the night. She looks back over the valley and watches everyone else leaving – the spotlights on now. None of them would work for the guards she realises now. The police would have been unstoppable if they could have enlisted the giants. She remembers how many of them had been at the classroom and smiles – none of them would help, none of them. That's why it was all so necessary. None of them would cooperate. None of them. If the police or the guards or the teachers had found one of them who was willing to be on their side, they would have utilised their compliance to the hilt, but not one of the giants wanted to go with them. They all knew the power they had. They had had power and it had been thwarted and now three of them have found their way here and, who knows, probably they aren't strong anymore. They had been forced to squander it all for the safety of their oppressors.

But now, they have no idea how big they are. There's nothing to scale against except each other. They know themselves so well in relation that it's impossible to tell anything from that except they hadn't grown in relation to each other. Growth or shrinkage is impossible to tell. If one of them is now smaller, it would be impossible to tell, in the place they were in, if the other two had grown or the one – smaller now – had shrunk. There's a distinct sense of nothing to do but also of there being a great deal of activity happening somewhere, out of sight, around them perhaps but not involving them. They constantly look over their shoulders thinking that someone or something will appear to tell them the next place to be. To tell them whether they're in a prison or about to be taken to a prison, because when you've been in prison, these seem like the only two possibilities. Perhaps they're back on Earth, perhaps they never left, perhaps this is a course in the classroom, it's all so hard to see. The place they're in is so without boundaries that it seems like every possibility is open to them. Anything could happen. Anything. They're silent. Like all the noise in them is over, used up, all the talking is over because there's nothing to talk about, now they know the truth. Drew tries to start a conversation about how they should prepare for the new place but as time goes on and nothing happens it seems like a pointless exercise, so they all just stand in the first room. Although maybe floating is a better explanation of what they're doing. When they tell the story to each other, trying to capture it for telling later, they're unsure. It feels like a type of gravity that holds them but maybe they're still falling or maybe they're rising up. It's impossible to tell but Alba feels like she's upright and when any of them go to walk say – they're able to.

The whole place gives the sense of waiting – for something big. But when it happens it isn't grand and comes from inside them. Like a thought. As quiet as that. That undisturbing. Just a quiet voice saying, 'Thank you for coming,' and then, 'Sorry for keeping you waiting.' And then a sense of a door, or perhaps rather a direction, to walk toward and a sense of something being prepared for them. Some other room, though the word room is a hangover from another place, another life. They move in the same direction and then they aren't alone. Around them are three more. The energy of three more.

As Drew, Stanley and Alba's eyes, or minds, get used to the idea of them, become better able to make sense of them, are able to see them, the three locals come slowly into view. At first it's just the sense of them, then a sort of blocking out of the space around them, so they come into being in negative space, and then a lightness and a smell perhaps, a sense of the warmth of them, the temperature change and then the sound of them, some sort of pulse, or a thing Alba can only make sense of as a pulse, and then the sound of their bodies in movement, although they're standing still, the sound of hair growing perhaps, or the way the skin sheds because all of it makes a noise that no one notices until it all becomes from nothing again. And then the locals' shape makes more sense. They're the same height as the three from Earth. They're covered in skin and hair grows from their heads. And Alba thinks, 'Maybe this is just a way to make us feel at home, because they shimmer as if holding a shape like ours.' They're slightly off but so Earthling-shaped. Earthling-shaped but in a performative way. Long limbs and eyes slightly too big and giving a sense of getting used to their mouths – not quite knowing where to put them, what to do with them, how to set them.

One of them reaches out and touches Drew's arm, Drew turns to them and they smile. Drew smiles back. The mirroring is deep inside all of their genes. The others smile. And then the conversation continues as if it's coming from somewhere else but the locals move their mouths to make it feel like they're saying the words. It's an odd feeling.

'We are happy you are here,' one of them says and as they

speak, along these lines – words of welcome, words of love – a world comes into view around them, is formed out of the many-coloured light. They're in a room and the 'roomness' of it makes Alba realise again how wrong they were calling the first place 'a room'. The large walls of the room go so high. The roof is arched. There doesn't seem to be a straight line anywhere. No corners. And Stanley thinks to himself, 'The aliens are fucking Steiner,' and Alba hears it and when she looks at Drew she can see that Drew hears it. The locals make a face like laughing and a chuckling noise but Alba isn't sure they get Stanley's joke. Because, although he's book smart he has it wrong. 'We are the aliens,' Alba thinks. And as she thinks it Stanley looks at her and she realises the noise of everything is in Alba's head. At first it sounds like it's coming from another room but it's coming from deep inside her. The locals continue to move their mouths and Alba is yet to speak but all the noise of the place comes from inside her and all the noise inside her is broadcast. Maybe it will stop but for now all the sound of the place is inside her and all the noise of her is leaking into the inside of all of them.

Alba feels the noise of Drew, in particular, being very suspicious. The static of Drew's fear playing with the hum of sadness Alba feels when she thinks that it might stop. A response comes, or perhaps it's a renewed confidence in Alba herself, that it's never going to stop – that all the noise of the place will be inside them forever. It is a bug in the system, or a feature. There's something cosy about it. Alba can feel the noise of all of them, their words, their breathing, the noise they make when they move, the noise their thinking makes. Like it bubbles up from deep water deep inside them and it makes the inside of them seem big – infinite. And she can feel the noise of all of them feeling this. One of the locals says, 'Are you hungry?' and a blush quietly beats in Alba's cheeks that all six of them feel. Her lips swell in a very small and slight way and she realises that only she is feeling it, that perhaps it is fading and she feels incredibly alone for a second.

Her hunger is a different story. She hears it bouncing and amplifying with the hunger all the others are feeling. She's hungrier than she's been in a very long time. The new sense seems to magnify everything. She's hungrier and when she walks she is walkier. Every part of her is ringing out with the noise of everyone else. They're all inside her and she's inside all of them although maybe inside and outside are pointless at this stage. She feels around and decides there's still an inside and an outside. She's like a wave in an ocean. It's a cliché but things become a cliché because they're true.

She's fallen behind and she runs up to one of the locals, the running is a joy and she forgets what motivated her and keeps jogging past everyone and with a full-hearted laugh she stops herself and runs back. When she reaches them, she doesn't want to stop so she jogs on the spot and at walking speed next to them and it feels amazing. She can't be completely sure she won't come. It's like everything she does is arousing. But she slows her jog, almost groaning with the sadness of it and says, 'Where are we going?'

And the answer comes, 'For some food.'

'What sort of food do you like?' she asks and the three locals laugh somewhere. They're out of the huge second room now and walking through plants. There's a gentle warm breeze which is touching her face as well. It's hard to concentrate she just wants to let the pleasure take her, the comfort, but she tries.

'Same as you.'

Alba makes the sound of 'That seems unlikely' inside her, to see if that's impolite but none of the locals seem to miss a beat or show any kind of annoyance. Although, how would she know? They could be priming her for battle right now. Maybe a laugh is the way to call an assassination.

'It does,' one of them agrees. 'But it's been prepared. We like what you like.'

'Name something,' Alba hums, and Drew hits her lightly on the arm. The whole place is pleasure.

'Pasta?' the locals suggest. 'Lasagne?'

Alba realises immediately the flaw in her questioning. It has been so long since she's eaten anything she enjoys that she has no idea if this is a correct answer. Lasagne is a thing, obviously she knows that. She'd seen it on television and also sometimes they would get small squares of crumbed and deep-fried lasagne in the prison and that seemed nice. So maybe the local is telling the truth.

'What's your names?' Alba asks.

'A.J.,' comes from one of them. This one is wearing a baby blue T-shirt with a hand-drawn animal like none Alba has ever seen. And the animal makes her look down and she is wearing a T-shirt that has words on it she can't read and trousers of the softest corduroy and she looks at Stanley and he has a T-shirt with different coloured spots and the same trousers in a different colour and Drew is in a T-shirt with a palm tree next to some water that Alba recognises as one from a gift shop, bought on holiday and given to Drew by someone who loved her enough to think of her while they were on holiday. The clothes are incredibly comfortable and move as they move with no resistance or pinching.

'T.J.' The next local down the line has long hair which is pulled up in a ponytail.

'R.J.,' the last local places an open palm on a chest. Alba, Drew and Stanley look at them now. Take it all in, so they won't have to ask again. Alba's hand brushes past Stanley's, and it's electric and she's sure Stanley feels it too because he follows her hand slightly as it goes away trying to hold the sensation longer. Alba looks and Stanley has a wide grin on his face and then she looks at Drew and Drew has the same grin. The smiles are not for Alba, they are private and for themselves.

'Do you like lasagne?' Alba asks Stanley and Drew. The three of them are still speaking with their mouths – forgetting they don't need to. The additional noise of their voices reverberates in them as they speak, making their cheeks sing and their chests boom in ways that take their breath away.

Stanley and Drew nod. Of course they would know. Alba stops and tries not to think that – think how Stanley and Drew know about lasagne. Tries not to think meanness. Not wanting that on display with everything else. But as she feels around and looks at Drew and Stanley she realises they're not paying any attention. It isn't as straight forward as everything being on display evenly, there's a reception element to it, an attention that's needed and Drew and Stanley seem to have very little interest in Alba. They seem to be dealing with getting to know themselves again. Reconciling and readjusting what they believe about themselves with the things they now know about themselves.

'What are your names?' T.J. says.

'I thought you were waiting for us?' Alba says.

'I said we were prepared,' T.J. says.

'For what?' Stanley says.

'Invasion,' A.J. says. 'Attack.' A.J. is smiling broadly in a way that looks, to Alba, like a misunderstanding of what's being said. A.J. puts a hand on Alba's shoulder and says, 'No. I understand exactly what I'm saying. Our world is in a place that pulls all things to us. We're always . . . we've been prepared from the beginning.'

'You'll get none of that from us,' Drew says.

A.J. looks at R.J., and then T.J. says, 'We'll see.'

'Just for future reference,' Drew says, she's touching the trees they pass, the leaves are soft and warm, 'this is probably not going to work.'

'What,' T.J. says.

'Welcome,' Drew says. 'Comfort.'

'Why?' R.J. says.

'The people who sent us, from where we're from. They will probably eat you alive if you give them any room at all.'

'Well, they haven't come here. You have.'

'No,' Alba says. 'Yes.'

T.J., R.J. and A.J. look at her – deeply look – listen from inside her.

'We,' Drew points between Stanley and Alba and herself. 'We're kind of desperate. Like, um, we're the bottom,' she puts her hand low to the ground, 'like, as far as power goes.' The locals are looking at her with such attention and care that it feels to Alba like she's never seen anyone hear anyone before. 'We have – none.'

A.J. and R.J. nod. T.J. understands as well but makes a small noise of agreement instead of nodding.

'Yeah. We're kind of very low.'

'Oh,' R.J. says. 'We'll see.'

'Sorry?' Drew says.

'We'll see.'

'But,' Stanley is trying to find a better way to explain it. 'We're nothing.'

'Well,' T.J. says. 'Let's hope so.'

'No,' Stanley says. 'No. You don't understand. What you want. If you want peace, a treaty – we're of no use. You need to be careful. We're the first but soon,' – he looks above him at the sky as if trying to find where they have come from and indicate toward it – 'soon they'll come. Looking for us because we broke their ship. Did we break their ship?' The locals nod like it's good news. 'And they will not want peace.'

'Oh,' R.J. says. 'No. We're safe. We don't need to negotiate – this isn't a negotiation.'

'And' – Alba had to say it, because the locals didn't seem to understand – 'like, speaking for myself, I can't totally guarantee this will work for me. I'm not a good person.'

The locals nod, their faces are serious now, they're listening and considering then one of them says, 'What won't work?'

'This . . .' – Alba looks about, everything about the place is kind and comforting – '. . . welcome. This place. Like, I've done very bad things to maintain the tiniest degree of the comfort that I feel right now.'

Stanley and Drew nod in agreement Alba is sure but also, possibly, to indicate they also have done bad things.

'Okay,' T.J. says. 'We'll see.'

'I don't think I'm going to change,' Alba says. They just didn't seem to understand. 'Like no matter how kind you are. I cut people who are kind.'

'I think,' says R.J., 'this is not what you think it is.'

And the conversation ends, and they all just walk.

Alba notices it getting quieter, or perhaps the location and quality of the sound is shifting. There's less thought in it now. More and more noise seems to come from the thing that's making the noise. She can hear a scrunch under her feet as she takes each step.

The sound of everyone's thoughts is slipping away, so Alba's surprised when Stanley says, 'Wait.' He doesn't stop walking but she can see him going over something in his mind and she has no access to it. 'We're big,' he says. 'That's the one thing we have – we're bigger than the other people on our planet. If you are as big as us, you will be big too. So, we can help you defend yourselves.'

'We are small,' T.J. says. 'That's why they sent us to walk with you. Because you are also small compared with other things here.'

'But we were told we were too big,' Drew says.

'Oh,' T.J. looks at the others. 'Then' – thinking about it for a moment – 'then, I guess you were lied to.'

'Wow,' R.J. says, in a jeepers kind of way. 'Unless.' Then, 'No.' Then again, 'Wow.'

'You should kill us now,' Alba says.

'You have a high opinion of yourself and the harm you can do here,' R.J. says.

A city is opening up around them. The sky is the same mix of peach and blue that the first room had been. There are the softest clouds slowly moving across the wide breech above them. Stanley has stopped and is just looking up, which no one seems very concerned with. The buildings are high around them and again, there are no straight lines. They're soft and labial and float – everything seems to take its strength from its softness. The light has changed slightly and Alba has a very real sense of the locals being in disguise and her respect for them deepens because the hint of what is under the disguise suggests how complex the task is. R.J. turns and smiles at her and it's a friendly gesture but also there's something in it that's designed to remind Alba she's alien here.

They hadn't covered what was happening now in the classroom – any of it. Mainly because the people who ran the classroom were arrogant. They thought they were the only ones anywhere and they thought they were smarter than anyone, like they had reached some kind of cultural and intellectual pinnacle.

Pinnacle.

Alba plays the word around in her mouth for a bit.

'Stanley,' she says it quietly but the locals can hear, although the thought noise is quieter, she can still feel them still inside her. 'Do you know this word – "pinnacle"?' It was the first time she'd said it out loud.

Stanley nods.

'I don't think I do,' Alba says.

'What do you think it means?'

'Like – a high place, the highest place.'

'Yeah. I think that's what it means,' Stanley says. He doesn't look at her. It isn't the reason for the conversation – for Stanley to look at her – she really has no idea where *pinnacle* came from, but she realises as Stanley walks slightly faster to leave her behind that she had hoped he might look at her. Look at her and smile.

Pinnacle probably leaked in when they were all connected and got stuck. That's what Alba decides. Or maybe it has always been there but there had never been space or need to use it. The people at the classroom thought they were the only type their type would ever meet. That anyone else they met would be below them. What is very important to the place Alba came from is who is above and who is below and because this ordering and valuing is everywhere and done to everyone, it seems inevitable that, when they were left on their own in their cells at night, it would follow them all there too. The idea of below and above seems pointless here. It's like the fall had stripped it out of them.

'Is this your place?' Alba asks.

'Yes,' they all say it at once.

Alba looks behind herself, 'Where does your place start?'

'At the event horizon,' R.J. says.

'We had forgotten,' Alba says.

T.J. is looking at her and nods.

'It's important that you know who you are,' R.J. says. 'When you get here.'

'So, the fall was the first room?'

'Something like that,' A.J. says.

'And how many rooms are there?'

'We'll see,' R.J. says.

'But we're here now, aren't we?' Drew says. 'This is the destination?'

'We'll see,' T.J. says.

Probably, Alba thinks. *I am dead.* Maybe the others had carried on. Maybe they're all crouched over her in another place, crying. Begging her to wake up. Would Stanley be crying? Would Stanley even remember? Was the remembering something for her as she died? R.J. falls back from the group, crouches to look at something. Alba falls back, crouching to the same thing, a thing she has no words for. 'Am I dead?' she says it very softly so only R.J. can hear.

'Huh?' R.J. looks up.

'Am I dead?'

'Not yet,' R.J. says.

Alba feels her face look shocked and then R.J. laughs, stands up and pulls Alba into a hug and dances her up to where the others are.

After a while, they're walking on something softer and it takes all their attention to adjust their gait. The firm paved ground gives way to something more erratic and organic. Although, even the most permanent of structures and buildings here seem to move. Alba thinks it's the wind, that maybe they move in time with that, like a windmill, but more subtle – a rippling, a pulsing. Like a way of getting energy. But then she realises they're possibly alive and like the inside of an ear vibrating. But they make no sound and no sense of the sound that's surrounding them. But not all sound needs her to be able to hear it. Vibrations acting on a surface could be silent. Alba, Stanley and Drew have fallen quite a distance behind the locals. *The locals*, Alba thinks and says to herself again. *The aliens have fallen behind the locals.*

Stanley jogs past her to catch up with T.J. 'Where are we going?' he asks. Alba can see, really, it's just to make conversation because really none of them care at all. Nothing seems to be bothering anyone. A slight breeze has worked itself up and it makes the calm the air holds more noticeable.

'To get something to eat,' R.J. says.

'Oh,' says Stanley. 'Yeah. I'm hungry.'

'Me too,' Drew says.

Alba can feel it now. Like the tiniest discomfort that doesn't go away like it had in the previous places. Then she stops.

'We didn't bring anything to share,' Alba says.

'Oh,' R.J. stops, and looks at the others and they all make faces like they're thinking. 'Maybe you can help with the cleaning up?'

'We can definitely do that,' Alba says. 'We would like that.'

'Excellent,' says T.J.

'It feels like we can work anything out,' Stanley says. 'I feel like my brain is relaxing. It was tight and small but as we're walking my consciousness is widening, taking it all in.'

The sky is changing slightly.

'Will this be an evening meal?' Drew asks.

The three locals look at them and it's the first time there's some confusion.

'Will it be dark soon?' Stanley offers.

'Oh,' R.J. says. 'Night.' To the three from Earth in the first instance but also to the other two locals. So, everyone nods.

'Yes,' and the three from this place look up at the sky and turn around slightly like they're making a study of the air and the atmosphere. 'Maybe.'

'Did you make all this for us?' Drew asks.

'No,' A.J. says.

'You're here,' T.J. says. 'And we would have no need for this place if you weren't. So, it's more for us than you and also, we didn't make it.'

'We just came to it,' R.J. says.

'As the smallest,' Stanley says.

'As the ones who were the right size,' A.J. says.

'To greet us.'

'To walk with you,' T.J. says.

'Oh,' Alba says. 'I see.'

'Probably not,' T.J. says. 'With all due respect.'

'It's not what you think it is,' R.J. says.

'Oh,' says Alba. 'That's totally fine. No one is ever really happy to see us. We're often a bit of a disappointment. Well, at least—' and she feels out into the others to make sure she's okay to carry on speaking for all of them and Drew and Stanley nod for her to go on because what she's saying applies to all of them. The checking is only habit because Alba can feel the boundaries are still leaking, like, really it's impossible for her to do anything wrong accidentally here. 'We're not what most people want. When we were small – we have grown you see – when we were small we were not good news it appears, or rather, we have just remembered, and then when we got big –

big for Earth you understand – we were even less good news.'

'It's important you know who you are,' R.J. says.

They're walking through a herd of small and beautiful animals now. Smaller than them, unthreatening. Soft and floating somehow rather than standing on the fragrant ground.

'Are you sure you're prepared for war?' Drew says.

'I think possibly,' Stanley says, 'we've been prepared for war. I think we're the attack you've been preparing for.'

'We'll see,' R.J. says.

'Is that a threat?' Alba says.

'Oh. No,' R.J. says. 'We're of no threat to you. It's a promise.'

'Everything keeps changing,' Drew says. It's gradual but Alba sees she's right, the sky has changed and the ground they walk on. The plants that grow around them.

'The way through is coming together,' T.J. says.

'We've never been able to rely on anything,' Stanley says. 'It's a super-power here.' And they all laugh.

The small herd is following them now. They have the softest fur.

'What are these called?' Drew asks.

R.J. shrugs.

'No one knows what we need when the attackers arrive,' T.J. says. 'We just come to walk with you and the way through makes itself up around you.'

Alba's suddenly conscious of the care she, Drew and Stanley are moving with – it had been there from the beginning. Like, when you tentatively walk out onto an iced-over lake. At first it had been self-preservation but now it seems they don't want to disturb the place. The place is teaching them; it meets them with softness and softness is how they proceed.

'Are you from here?' Stanley asks, maybe it had occurred to them before now, maybe it hadn't, but he asks it now.

'Sort of,' T.J. says. One of the animals is pushing T.J. forward slightly closer to Stanley. 'Our home is here,' T.J. says, waving an arm, 'but not here,' stamping a foot on the ground. 'An attacker arrives and they're met with a way through that doesn't disturb the rest of the place. It's a bit like an air lock.'

'Or a quarantine,' R.J. says.

'Or a vacation,' Drew says.

'Yeah,' A.J. says. 'And the vacation calls us here – the ones who are the right ones to be disguised in it and the right ones to walk with you.'

They are walking toward a field of purple flowers.

'Are those orchids?' Drew says.

'Bee orchids,' T.J. says. 'By way of an explanation I think.'

Alba walks close to one of the flowers and sees at its centre it's the spitting image of a bee.

'Our planet might be a shock – and we don't want to shock,' R.J. says. 'Shocked attackers are dangerous attackers. We're not sure you'd even be able to see it if you arrived straight into it.'

'We, also' – it seems right that Alba says it, being the worst of the three – 'may be a shock. I'm a terrible person.'

The locals nod slowly looking at her. 'I see,' says R.J., and Alba feels that they did indeed see. It's as if where they were before made it hard to see, but here it is clearer to the locals what she is saying. She feels a pulling away of the three to show they understand.

'You have responsibilities then,' T.J. says. 'You are of no threat to us at all. None of you. But if it will help you can be responsible to us.'

Alba feels a change in her walk as if something she is carrying finds a new position and sits well with her, with Stanley and Drew too. Some of the comfort from the first room runs through them and they can walk in silence.

They all look out over the land that is spreading itself out in front of them, like a biome in a video game. It's like from this new vantage point the aliens can see the nature of the place. The landscape being made as they walk, in response to them. As they interact with the locals and the place. The whole landscape bends itself in some kind of extremely complicated summing up. Making itself up in response to their reactions, to their questions, to the way they walk. To begin with, it had seemed firmly focused on their comfort. If something made Alba, Stanley and Drew happy, they got more of that. They had been naïve to think it was a welcome. Looking out over the horizon the three from Earth see it is more like a defence mechanism – a tranquiliser or a toxin made especially for them. Then they realise, the comfort happens less and less the longer they're here. The place is giving them less of what they want and giving them more information about itself. Like an opening up. Like a challenge of sorts. They are walking up a hill now, there's slightly more resistance as they walk, not a lot but slightly more.

The exertion of the hill ignites a small huff of anger in Alba. She's going to say something but then she feels the call of the responsibility she has been offered.

'Are you okay?' Alba asks R.J.

And R.J. nods, puffing, but still managing a smile.

As they walk, a stand of what looks like trees comes into view. It's as if the trees are coming into view but also like they're appearing in front of them, being made out of nothing. The trees are softness, the trunks are like a gum, paper bark pulled back in some places to expose the widest range of pastel colours, ordered in strata and sub-strata. The trees stand in a circle and are all very similar. T.J.'s mouth opens and it becomes clear and final that the locals are also seeing everything for the first time as well. Alba reaches out and T.J. tucks into a hug as they walk toward the trees all of them laughing and smiling. The leaves of the trees are of the softest, almost synthetic, fine imitations of some sort of pine needle. They flutter but there's no breeze, it's a perfect temperature and the air is fresh. There's no wind but still the leaves wave and as they do they change colour to match the trunk. The herd of animals as if waving goodbye nuzzle each of the six and then move away as if they're swimming. In the centre of the circle of trees is a large flat rock and on the rock is food in the exact proportions to how hungry they are and they sit and pass each other food. Leaning against each other, then as they become full some of them lie down in each other's laps.

'How long have we been here?' Stanley asks. It feels to Alba like they have been there a long time. She looks at the sky as if this is the place someone would look to tell the time – or the passing of time.

'Huh?' T.J. is running hands through Alba's hair. 'Oh,' and looks at the sky too. 'Not sure.'

They aren't hungry anymore and the place is a perfect temperature. Although, Alba thinks, maybe it's them who are meeting the temperature rather than the other way around. Maybe they're happy with what they're getting rather than getting what they want.

And this seems to make them free. Stanley yawns and then everyone's eyes get heavy and they all lie down and begin to sleep. And what will they dream of? Alba wonders. For they have lived so many lives. All of them. The aliens have been told all the lies and had lost the truth and then remembered it as they fell through the air, as they got away, as far as they could get from Earth, and the locals had been altered to look this way and were quickly coming to terms with the newness of the world.

in the work

Eventually they wake up and pass around more food and then walk.

As they walk, the city starts to come around them again and suddenly it is populated.

'Oh,' T.J. says, looking around. 'There's work today. Is that okay?' And the aliens nod, yes, some work will be good. It will be good to have some shape to the day. The day before had been nice but pleasing themselves will only fill them up for so long. The city looks industrial. The aliens walk along the streets and locals nod to them and they nod back. There are a large number of locals and T.J. explains that some of them have come specially to see them while others have been called up today to work and are here for that.

'Do we look strange?' Alba asks.

The locals shrug. 'Don't we all?' A.J. says. 'We're so changed here, what is looks? If you get to see us in our house you'll understand. If the way through takes you to our house you'll be able to understand.'

'Ready?' Alba says.

'Able.'

'All the buildings are huge here,' T.J. says.

None of the huge buildings have sharp edges. They are made of the same overlapping frills Alba saw in all the buildings and like all the other buildings these ones move in reaction to something. Is it the looking? But no, it feels like it's sound. The buildings are listening but to something the guests can't hear. Soundless vibration. Maybe they are the vibrations of the outside, A.J.'s house outside this place, the parallel place where other things are going on. The place they might get to.

'Is this a test?' Alba says.

'No,' says T.J.

'But you're testing us?'

'No,' says R.J. 'We are not testing you.'

There are more bodies now, first a few at a time, then more and more of the locals, like R.J., A.J. and T.J. but also maybe not. They're all walking together now. The place is being peopled. Much like the land comes into focus, now the other inhabitants do. Stanley, Alba and Drew feel them as they pass by. The warmth of them. They smile as they pass, and the three of them smile back. They are outnumbered now.

There are no gates or doors on any of the buildings. There's no demarcation between the outside and the inside. They walk through them. The colour of the light in the buildings is softer than it is outside. From inside they can see the light that the frills let in. As they shift in the soundless sound the light plays on the walls and on them. Alba has seen this type of light in advertisements for holidays in Pacific Islands before the pandemic, before the Pacific Islands sank.

'It's like we're underwater,' says a local who is walking beside Alba. And Alba and the local laugh.

They all, local and alien, are becoming used to the hue and the way it illuminates their skin. The way it murmurs off them. The way it seems to come with a sensation and that sensation is a hum as if it lifts the hairs on the exposed parts of Alba's skin up. It's possible that it warms as it lights and this is the function of the hair-raising ability of it, to regulate the heat on them so they're slightly agitated. The discomfort is increasing but Alba finds herself adjusting. And when it's at its worst the responsibility helps her think about the others, about how the locals came from what are probably their comfortable houses to walk with them and about Stanley and Drew, how the discomfort is hard for everyone, and in this way she forgets herself long enough to adjust to the new discomfort.

They walk with the locals through the large busy atrium and find themselves at a factory, a long production line. Stanley, Drew and Alba are brought to a place in the belt where three locals step back and make space for them. The work that comes down the belt is slow and the locals on either side of them smile and show them the job.

They fit in well here. Stanley, Drew and Alba know how to work. And everyone works together. It's a production line so it feels, after a while, like they are all working as one. The aliens hold things up to begin with, but things grow. Industries, as well as organisms, and everyone integrates them and their speed into the line, picking up their slack, fixing things that come down the line from them. Catching the odd thing that falls off the belt as Drew or Stanley or Alba reach with the wrong amount of force and into the wrong distance from them. There's always someone to help. This is part of the machine and the process and it teaches the three aliens how to be when someone else drops something. Through the learning and the working and the taking up their place they are less and less alien and change more and more into visitors. They settle in in this way.

There are breaks and everyone stops and has something to drink and talks to each other and then they move down a station or two. And this too seems to be part of the machinery and the efficiency of that machine. The stopping, the refreshing. Some workers take their cups into the brighter light that is outside the confines of the building and they sigh and some of them shrug and stretch. A few sometimes run up and down. Run about, and the rest of them cheer and laugh and then they decide it's time to come back in and they reassemble themselves. And someone checks everyone is okay, not with a shout or a whistle or a horn but with a series of soft noises that go down and back up the line. The belt starts and they're more efficient after the break and the belt wanders on and everyone is back making and working.

As the day goes on, Drew, Alba and Stanley get better at the job and they find they can talk as well as work.

'So,' Stanley asks, 'what are we making?' And someone replies, 'Food,' and the three of them look down at the objects as they pass them by because they don't look organic. They're the same pastel shade of all the natural things of the place but they also contain the grey metallic of the synthetic things, the things that have been built – the belt, the cogs in the belt.

'But,' Alba begins to say and then as she looks up at the building and out of the opening to the building she remembers everything is made here so any distinction between built and grown is pointless.

'For the way through,' another worker says. 'The food is for the way through.'

'*This* way through?' Drew asks.

'Yeah. All of them.'

'Oh,' says Stanley. 'Cool.'

Soon it's the end of the working day. There's some way of keeping time that Alba, Stanley and Drew haven't quite worked out; it's part of a growing discomfort – the not knowing how much longer there is to go or how long they've been doing a task for, the lost feeling of being strange and out of step. But they put down their tools with the others and walk away. There's a shower room and they clean themselves there. When they come out their shoes are gone. Alba looks around and everyone's shoes are gone. The locals around her see their shoes are not there, look behind them and just carry on. Stanley, Drew and Alba do the same. They walk barefoot with everyone to a large room and food is served. The food is served in a way that makes it portable. Some of them sit with their food in the big room, others go outside, others put the food into bags they're carrying and say they'll sit with it somewhere else or later.

'Do you want that?' someone says to Alba pointing to something on her plate. They are sitting outside.

'No thanks,' Alba says. 'Do you want it?'

'Yeah. Do you want these?'

'Yeah,' Alba says. 'Yeah, I like those.'

'We'll sleep soon,' the local says brushing at the plants that grow short out of the ground they sit on, like that is where the time can be read.

'Oh,' says Stanley. 'Yeah. That seems about right.'

Drew looks around, 'Where do we sleep?'

'Where do you want to sleep?' the local says.

Alba understands it's not a test. The choices, the freedom, are a way for them to get to know themselves. 'I like it here,' she says, and without seeing what the others do, she lies down on the soft ground and is asleep.

After they sleep, T.J., R.J. and A.J. come to see them.

'What do you want to do now?' T.J. says.

Alba shrugs. Drew and Stanley don't answer either.

'We could keep going,' A.J. says. 'There's more by the look of things. But also, you could stay here if you wanted.'

Alba and Drew look at Stanley who makes a face that they understand and they both nod.

'Where would we be most useful?' Stanley asks.

R.J. lifts a hand to shade the direct light and more easily look into the distance. A new landscape has arrived while they slept.

'I think,' A.J. says, even though it's R.J. surveying things, 'we keep going. If there's more of the way through, then you're not quite finished yet. This isn't the place for you to settle.'

'Okay,' they say. And the six of them set off.

Alba stops. 'Should we take some of the food we made?'

'Oh,' says T.J. 'Yeah, that's a great idea. The food is helpful at our house. So, if we can carry it all the way through that will help. And if we don't make it to our house, if the way through stops, we can always just use it where you settle.'

So, after filling some bags with the small metallic food they made on the production line, they set off. There are more of them. Many of the workers join them.

The landscape is hard now. The light in the outdoors agitates their skin now and the air is heavier, the ground tougher on their bare feet. Alba notices it isn't affecting the locals in the same way. None of them looked unwell in the previous places but now they look more well, more themselves. They stand taller and there's more laughter and conversation. In response to this and to the landscape they now move through, Alba feels herself become less and less interesting. Everyone's attention is off them. T.J., R.J. and A.J. take off ahead of them and no one explains anything or asks what they want. Largely they're having to work things out on their own and as they walk it becomes more and more difficult. The whole gravity of the place is shifted. They're dizzy in it while everyone else seems to take it completely in their stride. Alba feels muddled. The place requires things from her senses she doesn't have. She has to use all of her body in new ways. Stanley falls on her, but she only has the energy to lift him back up again. She can offer no consolation. The language is changing too. She can understand less and less of what anyone except Drew and Stanley say, but also that is getting tougher. The air, which is so much thicker, must be shouted through and some tones just blow away. Alba looks back occasionally and dreams of the comfort they left but then she feels the weight of the bag and remembers that it will be useful if they can carry the food to the end and she starts walking again through the air that pushes at her, and over the ground that forces her away from it.

Then she lifts her head. T.J., A.J. and R.J. are in front of her, seated, and Stanley and Drew are beside her and they're under the tree where they spent the first night. It is changed. Some kind of autumn has come over it. Its branches reach the ground now and it's a different colour. The sky around it has also turned. Everything is shifting from the pastels into much more saturated colours. The brightening has been happening, Alba now realises, gradually the whole time they've been there. But now it's at a point where it affects everything. The whole world sings in the bath of the colour field that comes from the sky but the tree has definitely changed colour, it isn't an effect of the sky. The three newcomers who aren't that new anymore shade their eyes from the brightness but T.J., A.J. and R.J. look at them with open eyes, waiting for them to sit down. The locals are stiffer in their movements and possibly taller. They sit in a more anchored way than the first day they sat together. They are taking up a different space. Alba looks at Stanley and then at Drew and none of them have changed in the same way. No physical change has come over them at all. They are the same as when they first arrived. Which surprises her because her insides feel completely rearranged.

'How was your day?' T.J. asks.

'Sorry,' Alba says. It's still hard for her to understand them. Despite the return to the tree, they're still speaking through a different material.

'It appears,' T.J. says and then cuts out.

'What?' Stanley says. There's a slight panic rising in them – the panic of change.

'. . . is over,' A.J. finishes.

Alba is almost overwhelmed now with the motion sickness. Drew's crying. Stanley looks like he's going to throw up. The sickness is in Alba's jaws. Moving from her ears. The sky is so bright and now has a shimmer to it. It all drills into their squinting eyes like a migraine. There's a sense of damp and the air gets even heavier.

'At least,' A.J. takes over, tries to correct. '. . . leave.'

'. . . the end,' T.J. says.

3

So they grow: being utterly defeated by ever greater things.

- from 'The One Who Watches' by Rainer Maria Rilke.
Translated by Charlotte Simmonds.

out of the way through

The ground under them feels wrong. Like it isn't ground at all anymore. They'd been through a lot. They'd grown, which brought with it its own vertigo, or perhaps disorientation. They had been made to forget themselves in order to be taught to be away from Earth. To forget all the physics they had been born into, indeed the only physics they had known and then, once learning how to be in a new way, a theoretical new way, a new way that no one could be a hundred percent sure of, they were sent up and away from Earth. They had been asked again and again to adapt. They had travelled, rebelled, and grown again. They had crashed, perhaps died, maybe they had died, but they hadn't died and then they had been placed in the most comfort they could imagine, and they had walked away. To here, where the ground slips from them through their fingers, like sand. Everything moving.

'Where are we going?' Stanley says. They are all finding it harder to breath, the pressure on their ears is strong.

'. . . our house.'

'Welcome to . . .'

'. . . out of the way through.' Drew is gasping slightly.

'Can we breathe here?' Stanley is starting to panic, shift about, but there's nothing to fight and nothing to protect themselves from. The world is dripping like water down a wall. Leaking, streaking, dripping.

'The way through thinks so,' says T.J., speaking clearly now. Every word seeming like a farewell of sorts. 'Or you wouldn't be here. You would still be at the first place, or the second. It'll only take you as far as is safe.'

'For us?' Alba says.

'For us,' A.J. says.

The world around them alters profoundly. Their three friends, their guides, the ones they trust are also happening. At least something is happening to them. They have stopped moving their mouths completely and reverted to the internal sound communication they had first met them in.

The three newcomers nod and gasp slightly and this seems to accelerate the demise of the way through. Their bodies are all rebellion but also there's a sense that maybe there's no need to fight.

'It will be fine,' A.J. – it sounds like A.J. – says. 'We are responsible for each other, and it is under control, or at least it is not under control, which in the end is fine.'

It will be the last thing they will say to each other, and then Stanley, Drew and Alba are standing. Their feet wet, then their ankles, then it becomes clear they are completely submerged. And there's a panic and it's sure to go through them and yet they feel held. And they're surrounded by a garden of circular discs, quilted fronds, phyla and mud-filled bags. Some attached to the ocean floor, some floating in the tide. And maybe this is the truth. The truth that has been there the whole time. The planet that held the way through that held them safe. They gasp and then with a slow calm that is being spoken into them they find they can breathe and then there's noise, and they look up and there is fire, and weaponry that although they don't recognise they completely recognise as the aggression that is uniformly in every person they have ever met before they came here. The aggression that has a home in all things from the moment they have a mouth and a gut and are faster and called predator. And they look at their friends – like seaweed, like jellyfish, like soft corals, sea anemones, sea pens and annelid worms. And their friends move in the sweep of the water atmosphere that is affected and in tumult from the attack. But none of them worry.

Everything is in hand. Nothing can do any harm.

Something radiates out from the garden, the shell-less population. It's the food they made on the belt and carried here but now it's also obvious that the food is made in the plants, like seed on earth, and the three of them are floated out of the plants and as they float to the surface the fire stops and the noise is silenced and a great peace comes over them all as the food makes a way through and the attackers disappear into it. *It's too late*, Alba thinks. Too late for the Cambrian explosion, too late for predation, but missing it has made room for a different way, an absorbing a wrapping around, rather than a pushing into. The plants waver and are neither harmed nor exhausted. They simply carry on and what do the three from Earth do while this goes on? They are protected from harm and watch and sing along with the plants. *Calling Occupants of Interplanetary Craft*. The melodies swim. And as they look up they start to get their bearings and they begin to feel the gills that are deep, deep within them.

Where had their bodies been? Had they been in their bodies in the way through or had their bodies always been here? Alba looks around and they are the only aliens. It was no dream. All of them had walked the way through.

T.J., R.J. and A.J. are nested in a clump just out of Alba, Stanley or Drew's reach and the others they know are waving in the tide and the fire has stopped. Alba, Stanley and Drew are visitors. Excluded from much of what is going on around them. The conversation, the action, all of it is happening around them and they look at each other, watch their milky eyes through the water which has been whipped up and is dusty. Truly dusty, and they can see very little but the activity around them is palpable. The conversation is too fast and complicated for them to follow. It's like this place is not for them. They have come from a place where consolations had been made for them, they had walked through it, become as helpful as they could. Become as normal as possible to this place. As harmless as they could possibly be. Slightly in pain, very uncomfortable understanding nothing but with an understanding of the responsibility – knowing there was no need to speak. The conversation is not for them. They aren't being ignored because of any disinterest it's just they are no longer the centre of the world. The world did not move for them, this is not their world. This is a world for the locals. So they stand as still as they can, fight the float in their bodies and just wait, until someone tells them the right thing to do and as they do this they get a sense that they're already doing the wrong thing and are a nuisance and also they are a danger but still they are here and need to be integrated because even dead, their bodies will be a danger. There's no other way out and they're sure that somehow they will be shown, they just need to limit the damage they do in the meantime.

There are things to take care of and the three of them watch as they get taken care of around them. There's a flurry of action, they're sure of it, it feels like there's action but it's hard to see it, they can hear it. Hear it in the way the vibrations hit them, the vibrations of an action that looks like nothing. Alba sees that this is how they would be the most dangerous. By trying to use what they had brought from Earth, here. Every time they try the old ways they choke and panic and it endangers everyone else.

The peace rains down and everything starts to settle into an equilibrium. It's odd coming into the equilibrium for the first time. Having arrived in a moment of flux, Alba's unsure of how far the peace will settle into – like a swing, they're unsure of when it is still. Is this the comfort of this place? Now? And to their surprise despite being hard and odd and slightly uncomfortable there's a sense of rightness that comes over them as the place slowly settles. It feels like a swing. There's a sense in the tidal, the tidal is acting on the locals and also they are acting on it. They look sedentary and some of them are in fact anchored, but they have great effect on the water around them. It's immense, they are in control of their environment, they are in many ways the caretakers of it. Alba remembers the builders on their own planet, engineers, who move the Earth and change it, change the balance in the orbit even though very slightly. The beings that surround them are like that, but they build with water and currents. Not all of them are stuck. They are radiant in form. There's communication happening but Alba and Drew and Stanley can't see anything that seems to have any kind of function of speaking as they understand it. But there's activity and there's talk about that activity. The vibrations of the activity swim over the newcomers and the immersion makes them feel like they maybe can understand what's going on, like the way through has worked. It has somehow trained them but maybe it's just a sense of hope and delusion. Nevertheless, everything changes, and changes and changes and finally they are tired and wonder if this is the end of the day. Whether the battle is unusual – historic even – or whether the attacks come frequently. Then Alba sees Stanley yawn, and this makes her yawn and Drew in turn also yawns and it seems like all the creatures in the biota smile at them and settle the water around them so they can sleep. They haven't eaten all day but have they eaten since they got here? There was the picnic but did they eat anything at the picnic? And almost without thinking any further about it they realise they aren't hungry at all. They're just here. Calm. The water holding them – perfect in temperature, perfect in gravity, no force needed to stand and then sit and then lie down and rest.

They dream of land things. Of the land above them. They're unsure, in dream, whether it's the locals talking to them or if they're autonomous in their dreams. No matter where the dreams come from, they come and come and have the strange time effect that dreams can have. And maybe in the dreams their bodies change. Their bodies work in the water but will they need new body parts for the land because about halfway through their sleep it becomes clear they are headed for the shore and their bodies twitch and shudder, like the dream is exercising new muscles into them, new nerve endings. They're in such rapid evolution that they think, because the dreaming is so lucid, they will hardly know themselves when they come awake. And there's nothing to do but to float and wait. It's a strange feeling to know they will never have to explain this to any of their kind. They will never return. They had been sent to die. That's clear now. Maybe they had been sent to take over this world, as some kind of front guard or maybe no one that sent them could imagine this. But they are lost to their own world now. They don't belong where they have come from and they don't belong here. They are the only ones of their kind who will make it.

Alba searches around her body and there's not an ounce of homesickness. She misses nothing. She was born into the world and it was not happy to see her. This isn't her home. She doesn't want to take advantage or be any more of a burden than she already is here. They hadn't asked her to come, she hadn't asked to be there. It isn't a welcome – it's an extremely advanced form of attack and defence.

onto the land

Wrapped in the fronds of the life around them, Stanley, Drew and Alba are prompted to stand and walk, and they walk, under the liquid, one foot and then the other and as they move each of the locals touches them as they pass, like it's a parade, like they are saying goodbye – hello and goodbye at the same time and they walk. Alba is a little way ahead but then she stops and turns and holds out her hand and Drew catches it and turns to hold out her hand for Stanley who grabs it also and they walk and walk until the top of their heads hit the open air. And as they walk further up the sea floor they blink their eyes in the air because it feels like a long time since they were in any kind of air. Alba wonders again if the way through had been underwater as well. Maybe this is the first time they are making it into the open above. They blink in a light which is bright and wide – all white and bouncing off the things of this new world, not a shade of pastel anywhere. Stanley is in the lead now and the others follow him. They wipe their faces and it's odd to have their hands. Hands seem completely wrong in this place. Completely wrong. Their hands are a surprise. They raise them to their faces expecting paddles or the sweep of light hairlike structures of yellow and other tropical colours but it is their hands, the ones they brought with them from Earth and it's strange to be back in their bodies, for real, under the pull of a gravity.

They have trouble walking. Alba trips but Drew catches her arm so she doesn't fall all the way. Then Stanley slows down so they can catch up with him. There's an odd heat to the sun – more like a humid warmth. Like the whole place is damp. Not quite dried out, more than tropical. More than what they expect tropical to be. They have never been anywhere. On Earth, they have maybe driven an hour from their home, or three, at the most. None of them has been to any of the major cities of the country they lived in. Alba and Stanley were in a prison on the outskirts of one of the towns but they never saw the town. There were high walls. One day, back in the prison when they were still close, Stanley had said to Alba, 'Are we near the sea?' and Alba said, 'Are we?' and looked around as if she was trying to smell the sea air.

'I thought I heard the sea,' Stanley had said biting the nail of his thumb.

'Oh,' Alba said. Then someone from across the table, someone who had been listening because every conversation belonged to everyone who was in earshot of it, said, 'It's the road.'

'Sorry?' Stanley said. So much of Stanley's politeness and his education and his brains remained. It wasn't that there weren't other smart people in the prison. There were people with PhDs and teaching degrees and people who had owned businesses and there were criminal masterminds – which was a thing. But something about Stanley was unusually likeable. People liked him.

Alba looks at him now. This is why it had ended up the way it had. With people hating her and loving Stanley. She thinks back – the memories still seem new to her. The truth. She sees that now. It had been Drew that had brought Stanley into their trio. Drew had come to visit Alba in the prison the week after they realised they were both growing. 'You have a visitor,' type of thing. They never told Alba who her visitors were. That was part of it. The guard would often force a blow job out of her before she saw the visitor so it was sometimes a real disappointment. And that day she'd come round the corner, cum still skating around her mouth, and seen Drew and thought, *Fuck*. Drew had said to Alba, *Look happy to see me dumb arse*. And Alba had done it sarcastically. And as they sat there that day, Drew had outlined the plan and Alba was suddenly interested and excited for real. Nodding and listening and her face didn't look angry anymore. Then, she saw Drew's eyes look behind her. 'Who's that?' she'd said, Alba had turned round and said, 'Which one?'

'That guy?' Drew said.

'Oh,' Alba said. 'Stanley.' And it was very clear that Stanley was taller. He went to sit down and smashed his knee against the table and then repositioned his legs so they were to the side of the table.

'We need a third,' Drew said.

Stanley is handsome and maybe that was it. Alba doubted they needed a third and she said as much and Drew pointed to her broken nose and the scar on her face and Alba was caught.

Alba looks at Drew and Stanley ahead of her. The three of them had been in relation to each other in so many different ways. While they'd forgotten the prison, they'd built a pretty equal working relationship at the classroom free from passion or anger or guilt. Sometimes they laughed together, they usually helped each other. And now, all of it remembered, there was an effect of the one relationship rippling through the other. They seemed to be able to fluctuate between the two relationships in the way through, or rather the work relationship, the new one that had been forged when the forgetting was complete, was there very strongly in the way through. But now as they walk onto shore Alba feels all sorts of emotions rise in her. Lust, a deep simple desire to fuck Stanley and lust, a very simple, almost primal desire to beat Drew into the ground. Drew looks back as Alba thinks it and Alba thinks she can see the fear in her eyes for a moment. Stanley is harder to read. What part of him has come back? Is it the part that could never forgive Alba or is it another part that's thinking, after all they'd been through, what's the point? What's the point of not forgiving Alba? The fight is pointless here. Now, in this huge new stage they are on. What is the fight even for?

Alba's heart sinks as she realises what's happening; the hope that's coming back will do her in. So she tells herself the story that keeps the hope at bay. Stanley has no desire to be with her. What she did was unforgivable. Now, in this place where they're the only three of their kind, it's extremely likely he will fall in love with Drew leaving Alba to wander by herself for the rest of her life. And the simplicity of it is convincing and she can walk another step out of the water.

Their feet hit dry land. They're still wiping the liquid from their eyes. It had seemed like an ocean but there's a different feel to the water once their skin hits the air. There's no salt. Instead of the sting it's a silky, strange feeling and Alba's sure she can hear the water evaporating off them. Everything sounds. Drew and Stanley stop and look back past Alba at where they've come from and Alba following their eyes does the same. It's a farewell but surely they can go back. Can they go back? None of them know. Alba wants to try it out immediately, submerge her face to see if they can return to their friends, the only chance she has for friends. She looks at Drew and Stanley. She has no idea what they think of what they remember but they seem different. But she knows enough about people to know that it can just be projection. She's weird so they're weird but there's something different for sure. Stanley is giving her a berth which seems wider. Drew looks at her but surely they're friends. The image of running up the hill away from the prison comes to her, Stanley holding her hand laughing, seeing her again the old way – the first way. But maybe that was just self-preservation. But then why didn't Drew and Stanley just team up together? We need a third.

Stanley and Drew walk away now, talking to each other and it hits Alba suddenly that maybe she's already on her own. To be alone, this far from home, with the two people she's hurt the most. She watches them walk away and then Stanley slows and, still talking to Drew, stops looks at Alba and waves her toward them. Alba runs to catch up with them.

'Is there a plan?' Alba asks.

Stanley and Drew stop talking and Stanley looks at her, shrugging slightly. 'At the moment I think walking?' He looks to Drew for some kind of buy-in. Drew shrugs, which is as close to a yes anyone is willing to give. They're in dunes of a sort, the sky is bright but has definitely lost all the pastel of the way through. It's very clearly a white light that comes from a sun that's moving through the sky but Alba looks down at her hands and sees that the shadows are strange, there's an umbra to them and she looks up, squinting hard, then blinking and sees that probably the sun is slightly eclipsed by something else. The world around them is deep and saturated in its hue.

As they walk from the dunes, there are trees, at least that's the word Alba thinks in response to them. They will have to learn a whole new vocabulary for this place – a whole new way of talking about the world. Alba thinks, *The plants in the sea.* But none of this is true. None of it is right. The plants are alive in a different way to the way that word is capable of and the sea isn't a sea.

Now they are a little higher, she looks back at the water

again, and it goes to the horizon like an ocean but it's moving in an odd way, right to left rather than toward and away from the shore and in such uniform waves that she has to adjust the word 'tidal'. She looks at the sky. Nothing she knows about right and wrong will work here. They seem to have the gravity they need to walk but every now and then they hit areas with less gravity and it's easier to walk and there's a sensation like they might take off. They're passing under the tree-like beings now and Alba wonders if this will be the end of them, this habit of thinking the trees are harmless. As they walk under them the trees move to follow. Stanley reaches up to touch a branch as it sweeps with them and the branch reaches out to touch Stanley's hand. Then it taps Alba on the head which she smiles at. Drew tries to talk to the trees, in the new, inside-out way, but they are not for talking and the sound that comes back is simply smiling and the three of them try to make the same noise back. The ground is moving under their feet, it's covered in small pebbles, smaller pieces of what the cliffs are made of. Alba's worried about everything – that everything is alive and it feels, definitely, like to some extent everything is. She tries harder as she walks to do as little harm as she can.

'Are we just walking?' Alba asks. She meant it to sound curious but it's heavy with complaint – she's out of practice using her actual voice.

Stanley and Drew slow and Drew wipes her brow. It isn't hot, the gesture is more for communication rather than function. They're out in the open, the pebbles are covered in a moss-like substance that is a bright orange colour and maybe that's what's alive.

'I'm not sure,' says Drew. None of them are.

'Are you tired?' Alba asks.

They all think about it, search their bodies. 'Will we have to sleep here?' Alba says.

'Nothing's really changed about us,' Stanley says. 'But maybe not.'

'Are you hungry?' Alba asks.

'I mean,' Drew looks around. 'I could eat.' There's nothing to talk to, really that's a lot of what they're all doing with this conversation – reaching out, thinking out, trying to see if there's anything that will talk to them, but nothing replies. Nothing talks back as they reach out. They all know so little but they know they can't eat anything they've seen so far. Even the soil seems alive here and they have responsibilities.

'What's feeding them?' Drew says.

'My dad had an orchid,' Alba says.

And they all think about that for a moment, imagine it in Alba's mind, as if she's offering a memory from home by way of explanation. Alba's father, abandoned by everything, distant from everyone but the orchid. As if the story is needed to explain the idea of 'orchid'. They leave this image then, to think about the plants they know, like the orchid, that don't need to eat. That get everything from the air.

'You know what,' Stanley says and they all know what he's going to say but he says it anyway, 'I don't think I am hungry.' And they look at each other.

'So, do you think that means nothing here gets hungry?' Alba is asking for a bigger reason than interest. Since she got here, since the crash really, maybe even in that hidden part of her back at the classroom, she's been afraid something would eat her. She's been slightly tense in preparation for it as they walk. Ready. Ready. Snapping around with every sound or every change in the atmosphere but maybe Stanley is right. Maybe nothing will eat them here because nothing is hungry. She thinks about that for a moment. Maybe it's okay for now to believe that's true. Just so she can walk without the distraction of fear. Maybe this is the best way to die. Unexpecting. Realistically it's probably all she wants. To go surprised and quickly and surely it would be quick. She's seen animals eat other living things back at home and it's very quick. Alba sees her own place in it all. That she too, back on Earth, had wanted to eat and food was scarce and that was probably why she attacked Drew. Scarcity. She needed to overpower her to get what it was she wanted. And then she sees the possibilities of not needing anything.

Suddenly there's a noise, an outside noise, and they all look at the sky where it's coming from and a terrifying armada appears. It darkens the sky and everything around them also turns to face it and the same attack or defence they witnessed under the liquid takes place. All around them seeds are released and they are in a snow of soft white fluff. The unknowable way everything on the planet fights back and the armada fires down but nothing hits. The basic physics of it is new to them. The ships fire down an arsenal but it slows and dissipates before it hits any part of the planet. And then slowly the ships disappear into a way through – their own way through, one designed especially for the soldiers on the ship. Not a drop of blood spills. It's as if the ships are disbelieved away. Deemed somehow unnecessary, unwanted and simply ceased to be there. There's no force in it. On paper the planet looks like a perfect target, there seems to be no predation which means no need to build shells or teeth or claws or any kind of technology to fight and maybe this is why the attacks are so frequent but there's something completely impenetrable about the place. It's impossible to get there without passing through the way through and nothing gets any further through than the place they are at their least harmless. It seems to be a flawless plan and Alba realises it is technology, it's not some quirk of the planet. The defence system, because it did now seem to be that, had been designed, planned and engineered by the underwater locals. Coming from here, being grown by the land itself, it was the perfect technology, the perfect solution – the only one that could last. The only one that would work.

'Do you think we're the only Earthlings here?' Alba says. They're walking up another hill, none of them tired yet. When they find themselves flagging they just need to stop for a second to recharge themselves.

'I hope so,' Stanley says and Drew looks over at him and Alba thinks it looks like they are sharing something very special and it breaks her heart slightly. It will be hard to carry on if this is the part she's going to play. She wants to talk about it but it seems like no one is ready for that. It takes energy to keep it private but she's able to. But when will they talk about it? They're just walking. Stanley reaches out a hand and Drew takes it and something gives up in Alba. She deserves it. There isn't a part of her that fully understands why she did it. She explained it a million times to a million different people, created stories about why she hurt Drew then using the same mechanism explained a million times to herself why she hurt Stanley but she doesn't fully understand it, not privately, not deeply. She looks out and finds her eyes full of tears. She pushes down the sob. What else is there for it? She acted badly – to both of them. Really, she's lucky they hadn't left her behind. To fend for herself.

'If we don't need to eat and we don't need to sleep' – Alba is trying to talk now, talk lots to show there are no hard feelings – to keep everything in the private place, not to broadcast it accidentally – 'what are we going to do?' Neither of them reply. 'I mean, I'm all for the walking but yeah.'

'Just enjoy the walk,' Stanley says.

A terrible rush goes through Alba that maybe she is the child. She looks down and a single fat warm tear escapes her eye and slides down her cheek. She will be very sad here. Nothing is surer. She's constantly discontented and this place leaves her with no distractions. She so wants to eat, or look at something – a screen, a fire. Anything. The temperature is so even, everything is fucking even. With the lack of danger she can feel herself trying to make danger of her own. She feels for a moment that she might want to die.

Stanley and Drew look so happy and calm and Alba doesn't feel this at all. It's wrong. All of it. She's wrong in this place. Alone, with her enemies. What will this relationship be when there's no competition for food or space or rest? Who is she if she can't even be happy here?

She wants to stop walking. Not because she's tired but because she wants to get on with it. Whatever it looks like. She wants to be in a place where she can see both of them and what they want. She wants to stop maybe to be oppositional. To try and force something. She's worried. They give her no reason to be worried but she's worried. That the rejection will come later and this is what the forcing is for. If she can just get them to leave her now, then at least she'll know where she is – alone. She suspects that already. Is pretty sure she's alone already. That even walking beside them she's alone. What a strange number three is. She tries to look away. Tries to act like she isn't noticing. They are both laughing now, talking in an easy way that she and Stanley never shared. Never. And this bores deep into her. So much of what she thinks of herself is based on what Stanley had thought. That he had seen her and singled her out and they had been together. And this is why what she did is unforgivable. She had said that she didn't see him. She feels like she will collapse, like, already there's something eating away at her insides and soon, when that's all gone, all eaten, she will simply collapse in on herself. And then her sadness turns to nothing.

She looks at Stanley and Drew again. They can't trust her. They're acting like she won't attack them, beat them into the dirt, kill them but she will. She's perfectly capable of doing that. Even here, in this peaceful place. In amongst all the calm. It's possibly the calm is what is making her twitchy. There's noise but it's all so calm. The wind makes a noise. It chatters around them then swoops and swoons. It's hard to be in the middle of. So hard. The other two don't seem to see. Maybe they don't remember, she thinks again, for the hundredth time but every now and then Stanley turns and catches her eye and she can tell he knows exactly who she is. Maybe he will hit her first. It's hard. They needed to respect this place but there's no compunction on them. Why had they let them come? She looks at the horizon where the other ships had been. They hadn't come for war. She can see now that that's what they wanted. The people in the classroom. They had pointed them toward this place. They thought by sending criminals, giants, if they survived, if they came in contact, they would get war. Even if no one else from Earth would ever make it the giants would take the planet for Earth. They would die probably but they were big and uncomfortable and full of hormones so if they lived they made a perfect front guard. But they are broken. The people at the classroom had broken them and that had been the mistake. Because when they remember who they are they remember who the real enemy is and, now, here they are, walking. When will they stop walking? Alba is sick of it.

'Shall we stop?' she says and stops in some vague hope it will convince the others.

Stanley slows and Drew stops completely, and they look at Alba and look around. Drew shrugs, 'It looks like as good a place as anywhere.'

'But what are we stopping for?' Stanley says. And they look at each other.

Alba looks at the things around them. Rooted in the ground things, things that don't look hugely different from the ones under the water. But they're sparse and definitely alive, but not talking. Or at least Alba doesn't have the means to make them talk to her. Maybe she's keeping so much private they can't hear her.

'I reckon we need to go to the city,' Stanley says.

'Is there a city?' Alba says, and as fast as it's out of her mouth she realises she can hear it. It isn't the wind at all. It's industry and population and society. 'Do you know where it's coming from?' Alba asks.

'Yeah,' Drew says. 'Good point.' And they all stand very quietly and try to work out the direction it's coming from and also whether direction works the same way here. They listen hard but it's better to feel it. That's what Stanley says after a while. Like you can feel the noise on your cheeks and the others stop for a minute and realise he's right. They feel it and walk in the direction of the sensation. And this is how they continue for quite a long way. Stopping, sensing, then walking toward the sensation. Over a changing landscape through all sorts of things that greet them, some more sophisticatedly than others but, Stanley says, they are judging everything on what they know from their own planet. They're still stuck on that. They aren't smart enough yet, smart enough on this planet. They're learning, no doubt they will learn but it'll take some time.

Alba watches the break of Stanley's jaw as he says it. As

he talks she wants to be closer to him. His arms are wildly beautiful. She wants to be close to him.

They are the slime mould here. No one here can work out what motivates them or why they move or how they move. They look odd. They look completely incomprehensible – like a failing. They walk and the trees and plants and the fungi and the flotsam that floats around them occasionally take them in. Muscle and contract and shift to be near them but also contract to protect themselves from their weight. When she first arrived Alba felt like she was a blot on the place. Some terrible parasite. But nothing they can do will hurt anything here. Not overly. They are powerless here. Wrong here. Alba looks back at where they came from. Did she want to go home?

What's there though? They never belonged anywhere and maybe that's why they can work with this so fully. Maybe this is why they made it through. Because they pose no threat but also make not a ripple. They will not damage a speck here. Or rather, the type of damage they do couldn't hurt anyone. Or maybe the damage they do is impossible here because it doesn't possess the conditions for them to do the damage. With nothing to fight for can there even be any violence?

Stanley and Drew walk hand in hand ahead of her, laughing a bit, and they turn and smile at her.

There's a sense of an end. Stanley and Drew are like Adam and Eve and Alba isn't sure who that makes her. It seems like there's no other story possible. And then, as if in reply, a light, floral scent sweeps past. She looks around but there are no discernibly new plants. But she can't really read them. Their individuality. The way they all live such vastly different lives. The shapes are so new to her. The shape of everything. And for a moment she sees the possibility of the shape of a new story. She isn't sure how to reply to the scent. So, she thinks back like they did at the beginning of the way through and there is no immediate reply but then there is and it calms her – bypasses all the parts of her that think and speak, that are trying to work things out and write the story – and hits her in her body. Deep inside. People talk about the heart but she feels it in her liver – the way she feels welcome. The permission she is given and at the same time the way of the place. The way she needs to be to honour the place. She steps more lightly. Notices the population around her. Expresses her gratitude and readies herself to be of use.

Drew and Stanley slow without Alba noticing and she doesn't realise she's caught up with them until her arm brushes past Stanley's. Stanley looks up and smiles and Drew, somehow seeing Stanley do it out of the corner of her eye, does the same.

'I feel like soon we're going to stop,' Drew says and then they all feel it.

Alba, because she's always the one doing it, looks back. They have been walking up slightly – so slightly none of them have really noticed it. The effort of it has been so slight it was almost unnoticeable. But they are higher now and Alba can see for a long way. It's breathtaking now – being able to see it all. See the way all the small parts of it they passed make sense in the bigger view. Stanley and Drew, following her eyes, look at the view. Stanley shelters his eyes with his beautiful forearm. The light is changing, a second sun is rising, one that's possibly older. That gives off a different, more diffuse light. Alba looks down and they all have two shadows, splitting off from their feet at angles. Each a different length. One sharp the other soft and round like the shadows had been since they came out of the water. There's time but maybe it has no connection at all with the rising and the setting sun. They stand warm and whole and together.

'Do you think this is where we stop?' Drew asks. Stanley shrugs and they both look at Alba.

Alba looks around. Everything so far has been Drew or Stanley's idea. Alba is not a leader. She knows nothing and then she feels it, that they trust her and that she can be trusted. She looks around and finally says, 'I don't think so. What if it rains?'

'Does it rain?' Drew says.

'I guess we'll find out,' Alba says. But it's more complicated than that. If they stay one hundred years, say, and it never rains and then they die and the next day it rains, does it rain here?

'Do we need shelter?' Stanley is asking.

'I'm not sure how we would even go about that,' Alba says. She's still looking around and trying to remember the way through. Where had they slept? And she remembers the stand of trees – the copse.

'I think this isn't the place,' Alba says. All around them are tall grasses for as far as they can see. 'Remember the trees?' she says – because that is the name they brought with them for the communities that had sheltered them in the way through. Drew and Stanley nod. They are quiet and then they all turn and head in the same direction.

It isn't sound in the way it had been on Earth. It's inside them. All of them. It calls to all of them. It's a vibrating. A resounding. And they follow the noise they had mistaken for a city.

Before long they come to a stand of trees who suggest they can stay. Suggest to the core of their understanding. Make their hearts see that they can do no harm here. That there's room. That they can be included. That they have not been here – forever, for the longest time – and now they are here and it makes no difference. Things change because they are here but in the sum of things nothing will change. They are that light on the land. The land is unaffected in their presence.

They aren't tired, nothing has been an effort of any kind, but now there is a place to rest they feel the time to rest move up through them. The ground is soft and they kneel on it and look around and then they lie down. Drew and Stanley settle into the cup of each other. Alba watches them as they move to get comfortable. The way the three of them are configured is clear now. One couple and Alba.

The suns are finally setting. It's getting cooler but Alba will be fine. The chill is a good reminder of what she's done. What she will pay for. Pay back. The trees above them move. It's an illusion of course. The paying for it. It's something that had been placed on top of the natural order of things. Forced into it. Pushed. On Earth it had only taken ninety years of the paying way and all the trees were gone. All the fish. The rhinoceros would be gone soon if they weren't already. It's like a meteorite that's slow and systematic. But it isn't even that – it isn't even real. They had shown that when they'd broken the walls of the prison. Even the prison wasn't real with the right kind of action. The order of things on the Earth they left was completely unreal. What she had done is true. She looks at the scars on Drew's face. Nothing that can be paid would make it better. Not money or property. Not even Alba's death. Not an eye for an eye. Only responsibility. Only carrying on.

Drew looks up. 'Why are you over there?' she says.

'Me?' Alba says.

'Who else?' Stanley says with a large smile and Drew waves for Alba to come over.

When she gets close enough Stanley pulls her down on top of them both and Drew and Stanley make room for her between them. Her face is up close to Drew's there's no room between them. Drew holds her face in both her hands and looks her in the eyes. Stanley wraps his arm around her stomach and puts his hand on Drew's hip.

They can feel each other now. The vibration that's distinctly their own hums out of them and into each other. Alba can feel it fully in her mouth and Drew says, 'Can I kiss you?' And Alba says, 'Yes.' And after she kisses Drew open-mouthed and crooning she turns her head so close and she is looking in Stanley's eyes and he nods and she kisses him. Inside him and joined with him then his cheek on hers and Drew's ear on her ear and they kiss and she is under it and reaching out for Stanley and finding him where he had always been and finding the pleasure in him and the solidness that is him – waist, hip, thigh. Drew presses, hard into Alba and hand on hand and then mouth on breast and the brush of another hand reaching and finding a strong upper arm. Mouths on mouths and ears and necks and the softest parts and the ground beneath them murmuring in response to their movements wrapping frond, blade, trichome in the tiniest embrace waking their skin, moaning through their bodies' speeding hearts, shallowing breath, broadcasting through mycelium and root to all the world back into the liquid and the liquid shouts back. Stanley's breath hard and short in Alba's ear, his lips holding her by lob and helix, deep inside her, tangled in her and Drew. Alba deep inside Drew, the ground, the plants winding around the parts of her hand still outside. No distance between them, and no distance between them and the place – all the other beings of the place and the things of the place pay attention, push in and away and in and away and then Stanley comes and then Drew and then it overtakes her and Alba arrives and arrives and arrives to find herself held and safe and seen.

Notes

1

The Donda West quote comes from *jeen-yuhs: A Kanye West Trilogy* (2022) directed by Coodie and Chike and although it could be read as a warning against hubris, in context it is also a statement about remaining grounded while you fly.

2

Avi Loeb's quote comes from 'What Exactly Is a Black Hole Event Horizon (and What Happens There)?' (2019) by Charles Q. Choi.

3

The quote from 'The One Who Watches' by Rainer Maria Rilke is translated by Charlotte Simmonds. Here is her full translation:

> I watch the storms grow in the trees,
> from days become sluggish and stupid,
> pound against my fearful window, rend,
> and hear a distance that never ends,
> say things I cannot bear without a friend,
> I cannot love without a sister.
>
> There goes the storm, a rearranger,
> through the woods and through the ages,
> and everything is timeless:
> the landscape, like a verse from the Psalms,
> is gravity and force and eternity.
>
> How small is that with which we wrestle,
> that which wrestles with us, how large;
> were we to be more like those things,
> if we but allowed the great storm to subdue us,—
> we should become vast and nameless.

We conquer only what is smaller,
and success makes us smaller too.
The everlasting and the awesome
will not be swayed by us.

It is the angel who appeared
to the wrestlers of the Old Testament:
when the tendons of his opponent
distend in battle like metal,
he feels them beneath his fingers
as strings plucking deep melodies.

The one who defeats this angel,
who usually refuses to fight,
they walk, fairly and squarely, upright,
tall, out of that stern hand
that cradled them as if shaping them.
It is not victory that leads them on.
So they grow: being utterly defeated
by ever greater things.

4

In the body of this work, several character repeat scenes and words of several romantic comedies. I imagined that when a character is called upon to retell a mythology it is the romantic comedy they enact. I chose these works because I'm interested in the way they are, by 2023, embedded in the Western, Capitalist cultures and foundationally, almost invisibly, influencing ideas of love and power. The scenes and quotes are used in an act of collage. I authored their placement in this work but the scenes and quotes themselves are the work of other people, as follows:

You Got Mail (1998). Directed by Nora Ephron. Screenplay by Nora Ephron and Delia Ephron.

Maid in Manhattan (2002). Directed by Wayne Wang. Screenplay by John Hughes under the pseudonym Kevin Wade.

Never Been Kissed (1999). Directed by Raja Gosnell. Screenplay by Abby Kohn and Marc Silverstein.

Gentlemen Prefer Blondes (1953). Directed by Howard Hawks. Screenplay by Charles Lederer.

Pretty Woman (1990). Directed by Garry Marshall. Screenplay by J. F. Lawton.

While You Were Sleeping (1995). Directed by Jon Turteltaub. Screenplay by Daniel G. Sullivan and Fredric Lebow.

Spanglish (2004). Directed by James L. Brooks. Screenplay by James L. Brooks.

Pretty in Pink (1986). Directed by Howard Deutch. Screenplay by John Hughes.

Clueless (1995). Directed by Amy Heckerling. Screenplay by Amy Heckerling.

Miss Congeniality (2000). Directed by Donald Petrie. Screenplay by Marc Lawrence, Katie Ford and Caryn Lucas.

My Fair Lady (1964). Directed by George Cukor. Screenplay by Alan Jay Lerner based on *My Fair Lady* by Alan Jay Lerner and *Pygmalion* by George Bernard Shaw.

5

The version of *Calling Occupants of Interplanetary Craft* I refer to was performed by Karen Carpenter and Richard Carpenter and appeared as a B-side to their Carpenter's album *Can't Smile Without You* (1977).

Acknowledgements

This book was written while I lived on the land of Te Āti Awa, Taranaki Whānui, and neighbouring Ngāti Toa iwi. While this book is not set on this land, I am sure my occupation of it influenced this book. The privileges I experience as a Pākehā on stolen land mean I have had opportunities not available to others, which means this book is here when others are not. There are other books which are not here due to the injustices of Colonisation, Capitalism and other violent systems.

This book is about the abolition of prisons and our present punishment-based justice system. In my personal life I am committed to this end and believe an urgent and imperative part of this work is Land Back in the hands of rightful owners. I send love to all people in prisons. As I wrote this book I thought a lot about the people I have met in prisons over the years and was grateful all over again for the time we spent in each other's company.

This work includes several characters with experience outside my own. In particular, I have written at least one trans-person as a main character. I wanted to write a world that reflected the one I live in and the people I love in that world. I am in no way trying to write a trans experience. The character whose point of view the story is told from is based on me and my experiences. My aim is to write into fiction the experiences I have loving and caring greatly about the trans people in my life. There are many great writers who write the trans experience and I am grateful for their work. Not because I have used their work as research for this, but because theirs are books that have filled my heart and brain.

I am grateful to my partner Brent and my son Bo. Brent and Bo are patient and kind men who bring me great joy and peace and excitement and laughter. Both are amazing artists and I am so grateful to live in a house that is full with the sounds and conversations of making.

I am incredibly grateful to the networks that support me. I am grateful to have Emma Hislop and Aidan Rasmussen in my life almost daily. Thank you for your love and encouragement.

Martin Shaw is my agent and has helped in so many more ways than getting people to read my book. I am grateful for the book recommendations, the encouragement and the patient ear when I am frightened and stressed.

A large part of this book was written while I was the Te Herenga Waka Victoria University of Wellington / Creative New Zealand Writer in Residence at the IIML. Thank you for the generous financial grant and space and company in the IIML to write.

Thanks again to the team at Te Herenga Waka Press, especially to Anna Knox whose skill and care reignited my energy for this book. Thanks also to Fergus, Ashleigh and Tayi. And thank you Craig for all the incredibly helpful conversations about writing what is real into what is imagined.

I am incredibly grateful to Giramondo. Nick Tapper worked extensively on the first draft of this book and it is a better book because of it. He is an incredible reader and I am grateful for his faith that I could express the ideas in this book better. Thank you also to Aleesha Paz at Giramondo. When I see an email from Aleesha it makes me happy. I'm incredibly excited to be working with Peninsula Press on this book. Meeting with Jake has been one of the highpoints of my year.

Charlotte Simmonds is an amazing writer and translator and I am grateful for her work and the conversations we have had over the last few months.

Authors I read while writing this book include: Jordy Rosenberg, Andrea Lawlor, Oscar Upperton, essa may ranipiri, Cassandra Barnett, Anahera Gildea, Michaela Keeble, romesh dissanayake, Laura Vincent, Kerry Donovan Brown, Emma Hislop, Aidan Rasmussen, Bae Suah, Sinead Overbye, Emma Barnes, Jos Charles, Mattilda Bernstein Sycamore, Hana Pera Aoake, Emily Perkins, Joon Oluchi Lee, Samuel R. Delany, Helen Heath, Helen Lehndorf, Rebecca K Reilly, Rebecca Hawkes, M. Darusha Wehm, Brannavan Gnanalingam, Sylvan Spring, Megan Dunn, Ruth Wilson Gilmore, Kai Cheng Thom, Victor Rodger, Ash Davida Jane, Rachel O'Neill, Alison Glenny, Isabel Waidner, Whiti Hereaka, Always Becominging. This book would not have been possible without your work and your examples.

I need to make special mention of Anne Kennedy's *The Time of the*

Giants. Anne's work has been inspirational and of great joy to me, and in a lot of ways *Audition* writes back in love and thanks to *The Time of the Giants*.

Finally, I'd like to say thanks to my work colleagues – Jonny, Tony, Amy, Gem, Kirsten. Working is an important part of my practice and I am grateful for your company while I make money to live.